TOOTHPICK LEGS

TOOTHPICK LEGS

To Dr. Bump-
Your class
was one of my
favorites!
Thank you for
encouraging your students
to write. Ashley Warren

Ashley Warren

3-9-17

Archway Publishing books may be ordered through booksellers or by contacting:

Archway Publishing
1663 Liberty Drive
Bloomington, IN 47403
www.archwaypublishing.com
1 (888) 242-5904

ISBN: 978-1-4808-3393-7 (sc)
ISBN: 978-1-4808-3394-4 (hc)
ISBN: 978-1-4808-3392-0 (e)

Library of Congress Control Number: 2016916165

Print information available on the last page.

Archway Publishing rev. date: 11/11/2016

For my family

SHYNESS

Ever since I can remember, I've been a reserved and introverted person, which, much to my chagrin, was known during middle school as "being shy."

My shyness surfaced just after the day I was born. I refused to be held at the hospital by anyone but Mom. Blissful only in the security of her arms, I erupted into screaming fits if she passed me to anyone, including neonatal nurses and family members. To my dad's dismay, the first time he got to hold me as a newborn, I let out a shrill cry until he passed me back to Mom in the hospital bed.

By the time I was walking, I could have been a body double for Mom's right leg. Anytime the doorbell rang, I latched my entire body onto her leg, securing both of my tiny feet on top of her right shoe and encircling both arms around the safety of her right thigh. She had to walk in that awkward arrangement to greet our guest, straining to lug around the extra weight with her.

In public, people would stare or laugh, so Mom detached me and set me beside her, encouraging me to stand on my own two feet. But if a recognizable face or a store clerk came over, I wrapped myself in the folds of her skirt like a curtain, not wanting to be seen.

When I was 3, our family friends the Carringtons visited our house one Sunday afternoon. I ran into the den and threw my arms around a tall pair of legs I assumed were my dad's. I looked up and saw George Carrington's smiling face. This man wasn't my dad. I darted to the downstairs bathroom and locked the door, spending the entire afternoon wailing while the others enjoyed pleasant conversation in the living room.

Mom invented a game to ease what seemed to be a case of social anxiety. She sent my then 7-year-old sister Robin outside to ring the doorbell. Robin pretended to be our postman, holding an invisible stack of mail in her hand.

"Ashley, say hello to Mr. Postman," Mom guided me.

"Hello, Mr. Postman," I said, fully aware that this "stranger" was my sister.

The next time our actual postman delivered the mail, I was back to myself, gripping Mom's leg and shielding my face.

That same year, Mom and Dad decided to enroll me in preschool at Hidden Plains Presbyterian School, just a couple of days a week. They thought it might help me to be around other kids who were the same age in a nurturing environment.

Mom drove me to Hidden Plains and walked me indoors to the classroom. She let me take a tiny purse to school so I'd feel more secure. Mom introduced me to my new teacher, Brenda Wallis, and asked me if I wanted her to hang my purse in my locker before she left me in Miss Wallis's care. Angst-ridden and fidgety, I snapped at Mom, only because I didn't want her to go.

Miss Wallis, who saw what happened, scolded me in front of everyone for my behavior. If she ever had a chance to win my approval, it ended right then and there. Something within me shut down, and I refused to say another word to her the entire semester.

During her parent-teacher conference with Mom and Dad, Miss Wallis reported the year's events, which included my preference to hold my bladder the entire school morning rather than use the potty in front of the other 3-year-old girls. Miss Wallis admitted to my parents that she wasn't sure whether I actually could speak.

But my friends knew I could speak. Fast forward to third grade, when my more outgoing alter ego came shining through at slumber parties at our house. My friends and I charged up and down the stairs, screaming as we chased each other on sugar highs and paraded around like supermodels in our foam hair curlers. My friends reported this to our teachers at school the next Monday.

"You can't shut Ashley up at home," they said. "She's so loud and runs up and down the stairs screaming at the top of her lungs."

"No, not Ashley," they all said, glancing at me for confirmation.

I sat as still as a statue, my ankles crossed like a proper debutante. The girls couldn't believe I had the teachers fooled, but during school hours, I remained as shy as ever.

I'll never forget the time Hidden Plains held a Mardi Gras parade. Every student was to decorate a Mardi Gras mask, the kind attached to a stick that you hold up to your eyes. A preselected "queen of the parade" would ride around in a purple-and-green float, wheeling around on her mobile throne doing the pageant wave. Mrs. Bonham, the computer teacher who doubled as our French teacher, shook a jar filled with M&Ms in front of our hands.

Reaching in, I prayed, "Dear Lord, please let me not choose the winning piece of candy. Amen." Then, I pulled out the one oversized, green M&M with a peanut that would put me in the spotlight. I imagined the hundreds of onlookers staring down at me from the anonymity of the gymnasium bleachers, pointing at my blushing cheeks and the perspiration rings formed by my sweaty armpits. I asked Mrs. Bonham if I could abdicate my title, so to speak.

Her exact words were, "Not your cup of tea?"

It was not my cup of tea, not my carton of milk, nor any other combination of container and beverage.

My classmate Amy Johansson was thrilled to inherit the royal title, and she waved and smiled so fervently that I'm sure those sets of muscles were sore for days. I, however, blushed whenever a teacher said my name in class, or any word that happened to contain "ash" within it.

One excruciating fall, the third graders had to recite a poem at the annual Thanksgiving play and feast. Some of us dressed as Native American Indians, others as Pilgrims with tight, white hats that made us look part nun, part cafeteria worker.

Worse than that, a line of the poem contained the word "succotash," which fell into the category of words containing part of my name within them. Every time we rehearsed, I could feel my cheeks redden to the shade of a third-degree sunburn, and it's a miracle that my Native American name didn't become "Fainting Pilgrim" after the performance.

I wanted to be an extrovert so badly, really I did. Once, in Coach Fiona Decker's problem-solving class, we took the Myers-Briggs personality test to determine our personality types. The first letter of the results, either I or E, determined whether someone were an introvert or an extrovert. I altered my answers to the yes-or-no questions enough to become an extrovert.

"Do you enjoy reading books alone?" it asked. "No," I answered, even though that described my weekends perfectly.

"Do you enjoy telling stories loudly in the middle of a crowd of people?"

"Yes," I answered, despite that being one of my recurring nightmares.

When I showed Coach Decker my test results, the lower half of her mouth dropped to what seemed like her shoulders, and then she looked up at me in disbelief, as if to emphasize that I was not an extrovert.

Years later, I retook the test and answered more accurately. My score revealed that I was 89% an introvert. Who would've guessed? Only when I learned that Mother Teresa shared my exact personality type, INFJ, did I decide that sensitive, serene, reserved, conceptual and idealistic might be admirable characteristics after all.

THE CARPOOL

The parents of 8th Street decided to form a school carpool, since there were four Hidden Plains students living on the same block. On Mondays and Fridays, Mom or Dad would drive my sister Robin, Kristen Bennett, Keith Powell and me to Hidden Plains.

On Tuesdays and Thursdays, Sue or Dave Bennett took their turn in the carpool, and one dreaded day a week, Wednesdays, Patricia or Danny Powell, who lived directly across from the Bennetts, drove us to school.

Danny Powell frightened me. His van was old and beat up and emitted unfamiliar noises. Danny stored his cigarette packages in the drink container next to the driver's seat, and the whole van reeked of stale smoke. None of my classmates' parents smoked, so Danny seemed like an anomaly to me. He wore faded jeans with a ripped T-shirt and brought a tumbler that emitted the aroma of burnt coffee. He sang along to the oldies station as we all rode in silence, until occasionally he broke into a cough, which came out like a smoker's hack.

Needless to say, Patricia was our top choice of drivers from the Powell family, until the day she announced she was getting a new car, just the one she had always wanted.

I was excited for her and envisioned the kids on our block riding happily together in a spacious SUV or maybe a luxury vehicle all shiny and new. What showed up in our driveway one day was a brand-new, brown station wagon.

I didn't want to offend Patricia, but I really wanted to ask, "If you can afford a new car, why would you dream of owning a station wagon?" But matters got worse, since Patricia ran chronically late to pick us up for school. Mom and I had a daily pattern. She woke me up at 6:15 a.m.

"Rise and shine," she said. "Are you awake?"

"Yes," I mumbled.

"I'm not leaving the room until you're out of bed," she said.

I got out of bed, and Mom hastened to the kitchen to make French toast for breakfast. I lay down on my bedroom floor for 30 minutes, until Mom passed by again.

"Honey, did you go back to sleep? Come on, it's time to get up," she said. "Patricia will be here in 45 minutes."

I didn't wear makeup back then, so I frantically brushed my teeth, combed my hair, scarfed down breakfast and slapped on my school uniform. Then, I waited by the front door at 7:30 a.m. for Patricia to arrive. With each passing minute, my stomach formed a new knot, which I imagined looked like those twisted pretzels Kristen and I bought at the mall. Mom hustled through the living room and saw that I was still sitting on the stairs, staring out the window.

"Is Patricia not here yet?" she asked.

Mom called Sue. Patricia hadn't picked up Kristen either. Sue called Patricia. It was a bad sign when Patricia answered her house phone. She promised she was just about to step out the door.

"The motor is running," she said.

Sue phoned Mom to confirm that from her kitchen window she could see Patricia's car steaming forth fumes from the exhaust pipe. At 7:49 a.m., she pulled into our driveway. Robin and I lumbered out the door, knowing we had exactly 11 minutes to drive across town before the tardy bell rang and chapel began.

I remember the first day Patricia showed up in her station wagon. It looked like a chameleon with its slinky body type in various shades of brown. Apparently, seating would be according to age seniority. As the oldest, Robin leapt into the front seat, and Keith, a year older than Kristen and me, stretched across all three spots in the back seat.

Patricia got out of the car, which I mistakenly thought was her warm welcome.

With a big smile on her face, she marched to the very back of the station wagon and opened the rear hatch, which exposed two efficiency, backward-facing seats. Kristen was already seated in one of them. She and I shared a look that said, "Is this lady serious?"

I went along with Patricia's plan and climbed in the tiny space. After Patricia shut the door, pulling down the hatch just in front of our faces, Kristen and I had about two inches of breathing room. I promise, a Chihuahua would have felt claustrophobic in that space.

Kristen and I dreaded every Wednesday of the school year,

now aware that we would be riding to Hidden Plains once a week in a glorified trunk with two sorry excuses for seats and a rear window that faced the traffic behind us.

Exactly four major stoplights, plus several stop signs, stood between 8th Street and Hidden Plains at 88th and Genoa Avenue. Mom didn't think the back of Patricia's car was ideal seating. What if someone rear-ended us, she wondered? True, that would place their car in Kristen's and my laps, but we were more concerned about the embarrassment factor.

While the rest of the passengers faced forward, Kristen and I had to make awkward eye contact with drivers and passengers in the cars behind us, which, from our perspective, were actually in front of us. We always encouraged Patricia to power through yellow lights, but she erred on the side of caution and never took our advice.

Keith warned us, "It's yellow," knowing Kristen and I couldn't see the stoplight.

"Run it, run it," we said, fingers crossed.

Instead, Patricia's foot slammed on the brakes. So there we were, face to face with another neighbor, Mr. Reynolds, paused at the intersection of 17th and Genoa on his way to work.

Again, at 60th Street, the brakes screeched to a halt, leaving us looking into the eyes of Evelyn Wallace, who fussed with the bow in her toy poodle's hair. Should we make eye contact or mouth a "hello," Kristen and I wondered. We always opted against initiating any amiable nonverbal communication.

It was like being in the seats of the front row of an airplane that face, in full view, the three people also on your row. If you weren't a talker, like Kristen and I weren't, it was best to just sleep so you didn't have to stare at each other for the duration of the flight.

At the intersection of 75th and Genoa, the last light before Hidden Plains, our eyes feasted upon the face of Luke Griffin, a grade above us and the cutest boy on the school roster. I could feel my face redden. Kristen and I turned toward each other and began pantomiming a conversation. What else could we do? Stare into the eyes of my crush and his mother?

Finally, we arrived at Hidden Plains. We asked Patricia to drop us off at the circular area of landscaping called "the corral," which was almost a full block from where our other classmates piled out of their cars. We didn't want to risk being seen exiting the vehicle with help from Patricia, who hatched us from her station wagon by opening the trunk door.

She was so in love with this car. We could tell by the way she beamed at us, her hands full with a mug of steaming coffee, and said, "Girls, have a wonderful day."

CHAPEL

Chapel services at Hidden Plains Presbyterian School began at 8:00 a.m. sharp in the gym every morning. After our parents dropped us off in the circular drive known as the corral, we reported to our homeroom classes to march into chapel with our grade levels. I absolutely did not want to be late to homeroom, knowing if I were, I'd feel 500 sets of curious eyes staring at me as I hastened stealthily into chapel, tardy.

Of course, Kristen and I experienced that feeling many a time, especially when Patricia Powell drove the carpool. We didn't see the exhaust from her car piping out in our driveways until 7:50 a.m., and with chapel beginning at 8 a.m. a sprawling 80 blocks from our street, we didn't stand a chance of being on time.

During chapel, students sat in rows across the gym floor with fellow members of our class. The gymnasium was an ever-changing chameleon of an auditorium that tripled as a sporting-events venue, a lunchroom cafeteria and the site of daily chapel services, where Monday through Friday, rows of uniformed students lined up across the linoleum floor. Robed acolytes walked down the middle of the center aisle, which was divided by rows of students who sang along to traditional hymns.

Elvira Burns, an older lady with a low, raspy voice and tight, brown curls in the shape of her hair rollers, fitted the acolytes before chapel in red robes and white overlays, which were stored in a small closet in the school's music room. Mrs. Burns was best remembered for her staunch Presbyterian values and her favorite declaration, "There are only a few of us Presbyterians left." Through the years, word trickled out that she snuck out of the administration building for frequent smoke breaks, and Hidden Plains parents spotted her on the red-eye, direct flight to Las Vegas, where she allegedly nursed her hobby of playing the slot machines.

On our designated days as acolytes, we had to get to school at 7:30 a.m. to prepare and receive one of four role assignments. There was the cross or crucifix, two candles or torches and a banner, which was a huge rectangle of material embroidered with the Hidden Plains crest that we carried on a wooden pole.

I dreaded being the crucifix because I didn't want to set the pace, and I knew I'd get nervous and walk faster than the melody of the hymn. I didn't want to be the banner because I couldn't see over the fringe, and I was afraid of tripping over the pole I'd have to carry. My ideal role was one of the torches, since they were light and easy to see over. I was pretty well balanced, so I never feared I'd light anything on fire with the candle.

But my last name started with "V," and I was tall, so I always had to be the banner, since our assignments were in alphabetical order. I just hoped my experience walking down the aisle wouldn't be as bad as the time when Maya Heinrich tilted the candle on her torch and caught Misty Gibson's hair on fire.

Misty's assignment that morning was leading the group with the crucifix, which placed her right in front of Maya's flaming weapon. Groggy students yawned and yearned for more sleep as the opening hymn, "Hidden Plains Is Our Joy, Outstanding in Its Field," played in the background. As I carried the banner, I tried to figure out whether Hidden Plains was outstanding in its field or literally out standing in its field, since the school was located across from rows of fields.

Just before the acolytes headed down the long aisle, Elvira got in our faces and said in her raspiest, most intimidating voice, "Don't swivel the candles," before turning her head to cough her smoker's hack. With Elvira that close, I stared at her dark, charcoal eyeliner and her tightly curled rows of hair shaped like small, pink foam rollers. Even as a kid, I thought she was only a baton twirl away from looking like a Broadway stage director 50 years past her prime shouting orders at the young talent onstage.

The acolytes' seats were folding chairs placed right behind the altar set up to serve the Eucharist bread and wine that represented the body and blood of Christ. All eyes would be on us during the service, and oh, how I longed to be sitting in rows on the gym floor like my classmates.

Mr. Tom Knutson, our chapel administrator, pounded the organ keys, thrusting his whole frame across the keyboard to hit the high and low notes in mechanical motions. Meanwhile, my classmates with less obvious seating arrangements spent their time scanning flash cards and studying for that day's biology test. Lucky them.

During the middle of chapel, students from different grade levels read one Psalm and one Scripture lesson. Students vied for the Psalm assignment, which was easier, like poetry, with short, simple words. The Scripture was more complicated with longer sentences and more difficult words that often involved Biblical names and ancient geography. Everyone was afraid of stumbling over a word like "Methuselah" or "Shadrach, Meshach and Abednego" or some obscure place in the Bible, which inevitably would be captured on a home movie camera by one of the Hidden Plains parents in the bleachers.

During more formal services, students wore dress uniforms, which were gray skirts, navy-blue blazers, panty hose and dress shoes for the girls, plus a red bow tie for added embarrassment. By the time I was about to eat the tiny piece of bread placed in our hands by the chaplain, I saw the cup of grape juice, which she wiped with a rag after every student before us pressed their lips to it for a sip. The juice and bread were a two-package deal, and the unsanitary nature of it all made me opt for the alternate blessing, even though my stomach was growling. I desperately wanted the bread, but instead, I folded my arms across my chest and accepted the chaplain's blessing.

It was time to return to homeroom, and as we marched out of chapel in rows, inevitably someone couldn't handle the combination of grape juice and breakfast from home. Within a minute, I could determine what the person had eaten. Clearly, I had a gift, though it remained uncertain whether it would benefit me in the future.

Usually, the culprit was orange juice and bacon or buttery

cinnamon toast. The smell was not nearly as sour as the solution the janitors used to clean it, which emanated the aroma of putrid sulphur and looked like salt sprinkled across frozen sidewalks after a snow. All of that excitement created a most memorable start to the school morning and definitely was the hot topic of conversation overheard on the way back to our classrooms.

CHILDHOOD FEARS

Growing up in the sheltered cocoon of a private school, which we called "The Bubble," it would seem that I would really have to search for sources of fear. However, this was not the case. Whether it was up, down, around or within, I could come up with something to cause me many sleepless nights.

Some of my fears were more rational than others. For example, I was gravely afraid of thunderstorms. We lived in an older home, and the floors and walls would shake and rattle every time it stormed outside.

Well, I was convinced our house was going to roll away with the downpour, our family never to be heard from again. I lay in my bed, one hand clenching my sheets, the other hand gripping the TV remote. With eyes glued to the local weather channel, I hoped and prayed for the severe weather warning to disappear, the minutes inching closer to the time when our weatherman promised the storm would subside.

Our teachers told us that lightning posed far more danger than thunder, but I had a strong fear of the powerful sounds that threatened to plummet my bed through the second-story floorboards into the living room downstairs.

My classmate Brandon Prescott II told us a story about his family's house being struck by lightning while his sister was doing laundry. The Prescott family installed a lightning rod on the roof, and at first I implored my parents to follow suit. But when I visited the Prescotts and saw that their home's exterior now looked like a regional storage center for metal beams, I excused my emotions from their fear of thunderstorms.

Regrettably, that was the year I watched far too much unsolved-crime television with my best friend Kristen Bennett, who lived at the end of our block, and Samantha Montgomery. The show featured profiles of criminals and heavily dramatized reenactments of their yet-to-be-solved crimes.

That meant these people were on the loose, and, as far as I was concerned, they had hopped the train to Texas and were camping out in Shady Oaks Park at the end of our block. I developed a habit of asking Mom to drive me to Kristen's house, which was a straight shot down 8th Street.

"Why don't you just walk?" Mom asked, so I mustered up some courage and headed out on foot. I started at a slow pace, but whenever a car turned onto the block, I revved into a brisk stride, just in case a felon tried to nab me. If anyone drove less then 10 miles per hour, I veered off the sidewalk so he couldn't grab my shirt and pull me into the car through the passenger window.

Once, a guy in a baseball cap was driving slowly next to

me, and when I glanced left, I saw caught his eyes, which then dropped to a piece of paper. Well, I took off in a mad dash, knowing that if I reached Kristen, whose blonde side ponytail I could see in the distance, I'd live to see my 13th birthday. Maybe Mom would feel such remorse about making me walk to Kristen's that she surely would let me have an extra slice of ice-cream cake during my next birthday party.

When I reached the Bennetts' house, I didn't even stop to greet Kristen. I practically flew straight up the sidewalk and into the safety of their front door. Kristen burst into laughter, chanting repeatedly, "Ashley's afraid of the pizza man."

Sure enough, the would-be kidnapper was a gangly high-school student, driving slowly and swerving because he couldn't find the right house and simultaneously was referencing the sheet of directions in his lap. Needless to say, our moms decided that watching true-crime shows was not appropriate after-school entertainment for Kristen and me.

At that point, I transferred my fear of neighborhood predators onto my parents, who enjoyed walking around the trail at Shady Oaks Park most evenings. Insisting they might be abducted or sideswiped by a swerving car, I pleaded with them never to walk at night again. When they did anyway, I cried and writhed on the floor to refocus their attention from their exercise to my bad behavior.

They responded by sneaking away for a lap when I was upstairs. They assumed I wouldn't figure out they had left at all. I did, of course, the minute I heard them surreptitiously close the front door, resulting in the quietest of squeaks.

I belted toward my window upstairs and saw them prance away on their tiptoes. I gave them hours of the silent treatment when they returned, though inwardly I was so thankful they were alive and not captured for ransom.

Most of my other fears were rooted in the fear of public humiliation or being the center of attention. Southwest Airlines had a policy that senior citizens and kids 12 and under could preboard a flight, even if the child's parents were on the same flight.

My parents decided it would be a great idea for me to preboard by myself and save seats for my grandparents, my parents, two of my uncles and my sister Robin.

They bombarded me with jackets, books and scarves to place in the seats and mark them as taken.

I'm sure they had good intentions of stretching me beyond my comfort zone.

However, it gave me major anxiety to think of saving seven seats and having strangers complain to my face that one little girl shouldn't be allowed to section off two-and-a-half rows of seats for her extended family. I didn't even like to talk to my teachers, much less confrontational fliers who all seemed to want to sit by me.

As soon as the attendant called out the preboard announcement, I made myself scarce, finding some emergency excuse, usually a prolonged visit to the bathroom. Thankfully, the next year, my grandmother became eligible for preboarding as a senior citizen. She was more than happy to march onto the plane solo and convey to dozens of travelers, "Sorry, these seven seats are taken."

Mom must have really wanted me to grow in confidence because another time, she purchased at an auction the opportunity for me to be a ball girl during a local, college-basketball home game. Other preteen girls would've wrestled each other to the ground for the privilege of rebounding basketballs before the game and returning them to the male players so they could continue warming up.

My other responsibility as a ball girl would consist of wielding a giant, rectangular mop and wiping up sweat and blood after a player hit the ground with a splat from getting slammed by a foul or shooting a wild, running layup. Did I mention that the arena seated 25,000 people? It's safe to assume that too many eyes would be aimed in my vicinity behind the basket, where ball girls squatted the entire two hours with clean-up kits of mops and towels.

In the end, Mom had to give the opportunity to our neighbor, Lauren Cooley. Lauren gladly accepted, doing a celebratory victory dance for what her dad Paul called "the chance of a lifetime." To Lauren, I will always be grateful.

But then my parents got the itch to travel, and it was time to tackle my ultimate childhood fear. The whole family was set to go on a cruise to Alaska with a big group of fellow furniture dealers. In an untimely twist of fate, we were studying the destructive effects of tsunamis in science class.

Once I learned of the historic 1883 Krakatoa tsunami, which eliminated most of Indonesia and sent tides rippling to Hawaii and Europe, I was convinced that if water were wet, it was no friend of mine. Even Kristen's waterbed was unsafe, as far as I was concerned.

Mom and Dad told me I needed to pack for Alaska. I asked them if they were aware that a tsunami can be generated by any large adjustment to sea level and would there be any heavyset people traveling on our ship? They told me we would be on the Inside Passage, which was the calmest, safest route through the Alaskan waters.

I informed them that tsunamis gain their speed in shallow water and can soar up to 600 feet in height. My dad said he had never even heard of tsunamis before my tirades. I told him they happened twice a year, the most destructive every 15 years. He said we were going on the cruise, and that was final.

We did, and I had a lovely time enjoying the gourmet midnight buffets with my grandfather and the Broadway-quality stage productions with my grandmother. Mom and Dad, on the other hand, spent much of their time seasick in their cabin after the ship's captain decided to make up some time by venturing away from the calm course of Alaska's Inside Passage in favor of the wild and choppy waves of the open Atlantic.

MOM

Mom and I became best friends shortly after my departure from her womb. I was a peaceful baby and entered the world after a minimal amount of labor. According to Mom, they handed me to her, and I was a happy girl. But if anyone else tried to hold me, including my dad, I started to wail until I was back with Mom.

Our bond deepened early. Once, when I was a tiny 2-year-old, Mom and I were walking across the street together at the grocery store, and an older lady who couldn't see well sailed through the parking lot in her large sedan. The second Mom saw the lady's car come toward my side of the path, she scooped me out of harm's way and saved my life. It was one of my earliest and most vivid memories.

Throughout my childhood, Mom was very involved at Hidden Plains. If parents were invited, Mom was there, serving cafeteria food, attending chapel services and running the concession stand during basketball games. She picked me up from school just about every day from preschool through ninth grade.

One of my teachers said she knew when Mom's Cadillac was arriving because in the distance, across the field from where we stood, she couldn't see a car, just dirt churning off the tires in a cloud of dust as Mom zipped onto campus at record speeds.

If I ever got sick, I didn't really mind because Mom showed me the utmost sympathy. "I'm torry you're tick," she said, followed by, "You're too tweet to be tick."

After a visit to the doctor, she let me select a package of cherry-flavored cough drops from the hospital pharmacy, even if my condition didn't involve a sore throat. Having a sweet tooth herself, Mom understood my affection for sugary desserts. She stocked one of the kitchen drawers full of apple fritters that tasted delicious with their fried shells, gooey, apple insides and white icing along the exterior. Together, we experienced the joy of consuming them and endured the pain of digesting them.

For my birthday party one year, Mom and Dad rented out Onward Leap, a local gymnastics training center. They watched as my friends and I bounced merrily on giant trampolines and tried to emulate famous gymnasts on the uneven bars, more often coming away with shoulder injuries instead of ribbons and medals. Mom let us go nuts in there until it was time for her to disburse the sugary fruit drinks in barrel containers and the personalized, frosted birthday cake she had ordered from Ms. Cinnamon's Bakery.

Mom made any activity lots of fun, even mopping the

kitchen floors. She activated the overhead ceiling fan, cranked up some gospel music and let me dance in the suds as we joined Aretha and Ella in belting out our hearts to the Lord.

Mom's favorite song to play on the piano was Jerry Lee Lewis's "Great Balls of Fire." It was very high energy, just like Mom. Back then, she was in a phase of salon-coloring her fluffy hair bright orange and rolling her curls to stand several inches above her head.

Looking like Liberace, Mom's long arms tickled the keys and in one swoop spanned the right side of the keyboard all the way to the left side to hit the song's crescendo. My best friend Kristen thought this was hilarious and threw her hands up in glee as we improvised new dance moves on the hardwood floors.

Every time one of my friends had a birthday, Mom took me to the mall and let me select a Joe Boxer pajama set as a birthday gift. The outfits ranged from blue-and-white-checkered cotton pajamas to long-sleeve silk pajamas overlaid with a yellow smiley-face pattern. Every selection had an elastic waistband that read "JOE BOXER," and my friends thought Mom was the most benevolent lady in town.

Another time, one of my friend's families was going through a hard time. Mom drove us to the department store and let my friend pick out a new bra-and-panty set to give her mom as a Christmas present. Mom may never fully realize how much her generosity impacted my decisions, both then and now.

As the family disciplinarian, Mom also had a business side, which we called "Business Mom," the alternative to "Fun Mom." Mom wanted me to attend Sunday school, even when I went through a phase of moaning my best excuse to sleep in, "I'm tired." Early Sunday morning, she switched on my bedroom ceiling fan and flipped on the lights, even the closet lights, so that they glared into my groggy eyes. Next, she stripped the comforter from my bed and blared her operatic radio music in the bathroom while she dressed for church.

If all else failed, she planted herself on the living-room piano bench and banged on the keys, sending echoes of her beloved Methodist hymns reverberating throughout the floors in every room. As the saying goes, "A dead person couldn't sleep in this house," and so we all rolled out of bed and attended church as a family.

Mom was a working mom. In the early 1980s, when Mom and Dad were in their 30s, they bought several duplexes as investment properties. Since Dad managed the family business, Mom was in charge of overseeing the rentals.

She worked from home, so Robin and I grew up on the industry lingo, and we tagged along as Mom fulfilled her professional responsibilities. Whenever a property became vacant, Mom drove there to post a metal sign that read, "FOR RENT." Robin and I got to stomp its metal stake into the lawn, which made us feel as though we were part of Mom's management team.

Potential tenants called our home phone number to inquire about the specifics. Mom always had the same pitch. "It's a two-bedroom, two-bathroom duplex with all appliances included, no pets allowed," she said. "We pay the water, you pay the rest of the bills." The speech was so predictable that I had it memorized, and whenever Mom restated it to someone in person, I parroted her response aloud while the other person looked at me like I was a real-estate baroness in the making.

I owe Mom a debt of gratitude for fostering my intellectual capacity. She paid me $10 for every book report I wrote on a challenging read. Mom graded each one, usually returning it to me with a 100% score and an inscription like "Excellent use of vocabulary. Love, Mom." Mom predicted early on that I would grow up to be a writer.

As a kid, I watched everything Mom did, including the things she probably wished I hadn't seen. When she stopped in the far right traffic lane to turn at a red light, she obeyed the law of braking for three seconds, but at her own discretion. She said aloud, "1,2,3," in a condensed, single syllable, her car paused but still in motion to beat the ones headed toward us through their green light.

Back at home, Mom and I exercised together to Jane Fonda and Jazzercise workout videos. Mom wore her yellow-and-black-checkered leotard and tights just like the Jazzercise lady, and I wore my patriotic leotard of the American flag, just like the leotard that gymnast Mary Lou Retton wore during the 1984 Los Angeles Olympics. When Mom did the splits, I stood behind her and winced in pain, vowing to eventually become more pliable. As Mom shimmied and swayed to songs like "Wake Me Up Before You Go Go," I mimicked every hip shake and high kick she conquered.

After each session, Mom encouraged me to walk with good posture. "Shoulders back, chest out," she said, to which I rolled my eyes, not wanting to seem voluptuous by extending my chest. "Someday, you'll bare those things with pride," she said, embarrassing me even more by beating her fists against her chest and roaring like a Viking woman.

Yes, you could say Mom and I were two of a kind, attached at the hip, which is why she nicknamed me "baby beans," "my little kumquat" and "darlin' baby," which she worked into phrases such as, "Well, darlin' baby, did you jam your finger in the car door?" I thought she was the most fun, most beautiful, most loving woman that ever lived. Still do.

I held a deep sense of security throughout my childhood because of Mom's unconditional love and support, knowing she would do and sacrifice anything to make my life better, and my sister's, whose toenails Mom clipped through Robin's senior year of high school. I think Dad summed up Mom's devotion best when he said, "If Mom could wee wee for you, I'm sure she would."

DAD

My favorite quality about Dad is that he is a laid-back guy's guy who is sentimental, not materialistic and answers every holiday-gift-idea request with "make me something." But during my middle-school years, I didn't appreciate these special traits like I do now.

Back then, Dad drove a beat-up Buick that he accepted from his younger brother Griffin. The car was already ghetto enough, but it had one feature in particular that drove me nuts. The material on the interior roof of the back seat drooped down and collected dust, insects and spider webs, leading me to call it "the nest." If Mom had an appointment, Dad picked me up from school in the Buick, and as soon as I saw the nest approach, I burst into tears. The rest of the Hidden Plains parking lot looked like a Lexus, BMW and Mercedes dealership, so I cried the whole way home, not because of Dad but because of the car.

It wasn't long before Dad and I bonded over the game of basketball, which he taught me to play in our driveway. We ran passing drills and scoring drills, and then after a good, long workout, he had me dribble 50 times with each hand as I walked along the concrete without looking at the ball.

During games, I couldn't seem to muster any competitive spirit, so Dad offered to pay me $5 per foul I committed. I sincerely thought such imperfections would appear on the permanent records our teachers liked to mention, so it was not a bribe I was willing to take. Even so, when Dad coached my city-league basketball team, I could count on his naming me the undisputed MVP every year. There was really no contest when the only voter happened to be my dad.

Still, the title was nothing to balk at because I got to amass a collection of miniature, gold trophies featuring a female basketball player shooting the ball and a tiny plaque underneath that stated my name and my sixth-grade MVP status.

Dad totally relished in my tomboy days that coincided with my interest in basketball. He took me to Champs Sports at the mall and let me buy a Michael Jordan poster and an Orlando Magic jersey with Shaquille O'Neal's name printed on the back. It was a sad day for Dad when I lost the perm, braces and glasses, instead morphing into a girly girl.

Even then, Dad put forth the effort to connect with me, so he drove Kristen Bennett and me to the mall, where he read the newspaper and drank sweet tea at a restaurant while Kristen and I shopped the stores.

Kristen and I had a pattern of calling in our food orders from the table's red telephone that had a curly-q cord, like a pig's tail. Then, we scurried away for 20 minutes while our food was cooking and bought multiple copies of the poem "Footprints" and posters of a single word, like "Courage," set into plastic frames. We came back and unloaded our loot on the table to show Dad, who always beamed like we had unearthed priceless sunken treasure.

We could count on his being the lenient, fun parent, and whenever I wanted something obnoxious, like a troll doll whose hair stuck straight up, I asked Dad, who said, "Yes, just show me that killer smile," causing me to erupt into a grin so massive that it exposed even my back molars. That same smile convinced Dad to let me get my ears pierced. He took me to Claire's at the mall and let me grip the bones in his hand as a needle-wielding woman approached my padded stool and drew a purple dot on my earlobes to ensure the evenness of the holes she was about to puncture.

As the woman pricked my ears with what felt like a razor blade, Dad watched me go from a girl who wore clip-ons and stick-ons to a young woman who wore stud earrings and thus needed all sorts of paraphernalia, including huge bottles of sterilizing solution and bulk amounts of earring backs, just in case. The man was a grown-up kid, and I loved having him as a dad.

On Sundays, when the family furniture store was closed to customers, Dad let Kristen and me bounce across the rows of display mattresses lined up against the wall. We screamed and giggled, jumping on them like trampolines until we plunked down, out of breath, and rested on our own personal beds.

Not that Dad was perfect. One year, during a parent-teacher conference with Mrs. Sweeney, she basically said that I was the perfect student who submitted everything on time and never missed class.

Dad casually referenced Mrs. Sweeney's newfound form of discipline and said, "Every kid should get her name on the board at least once," implying that I had a wake-up call in my future if I thought I could squeak through life perfectly.

Imagine my surprise and humiliation the next day when, minding my own business at my desk, I looked up to see my name written in chalk and all-capital letters on the board. Dad told me I learned a valuable lesson, that life wasn't fair, but I was convinced of another truth, that Dad wasn't fair.

Another time, Dad was almost involved in a wreck in the mall parking lot. We had just left the nutrition store GNC, where Dad bought me chewable vitamin C tablets that tasted as good as candy. Dad and a random lady, both of them weaving through multiple lanes, almost collided their cars. She honked, and Dad tossed his hands in the air in frustration. I was humiliated and let him know by slumping in my seat and turning my head the other way. Dad reclaimed the sack of vitamins by yanking them out of my lap.

Later that evening, he stood in the entryway of my bedroom door, where he pointed his finger and asked, "Hey, who loves you, babe?" as the loose skin around his jawline jiggled. That wasn't my idea of an apology, so I remained stoic with my arms crossed until Mom came in to act as an intermediary.

Once a week, Dad volunteered to drive the carpool to Hidden Plains, which I dreaded because he drove slowly and wouldn't run yellow lights. Judging by the way our car inched along the open road, I wasn't convinced Dad was going to run a green light either. He parted the Red Sea as cars revved by us on both sides, and I suddenly understood why the DPS posted signs with minimum speed-limit requirements.

Dad looked in the rearview mirror and tried to start a conversation with our 13-year-old neighbor Keith Powell, who wore his headphones, folded his arms across his chest and grunted incomprehensible responses. After that, Dad received strict orders from me not to talk to the carpool members. Years later, he told me, "As I drove along in silence, the only thing I had to look forward to was watching the sun rise over the clouds."

During those years, I was the only Hidden Plains student who didn't get to return my textbooks at the end of the year because Dad bought them from the school for his personal book collection. From preschool finger painting to middle-school history, Dad longed to help Robin and me with our homework, which he did until I forced him into early retirement after my sixth-grade year.

I'd like to blame it all on the preteen years, but in retrospect, I could have lost the attitude and focused on Dad's active involvement in my life. After all, it was Dad who inspired what I was certain would be my future career.

He started taking our family to the Disney theme parks when Robin was 6 and I was 2. Every year, we rotated Disneyland in California and Walt Disney World in Florida, and by his reaction upon arrival, it was evident that these annual vacations were not for the kids' benefit, but for Dad's.

He could have relocated permanently to the England section of Epcot and watched the Beatles impersonators, whom we called the "fake Beatles," perfect their harmony and sign impostor autographs.

One of Dad's greatest moments was when, at age 12, I

announced to him my dream career of working as the train conductor at Big Thunder Mountain Railroad inside the Magic Kingdom. I even drew a picture of myself wearing a train conductor's uniform, pulling the lever to start the ride with reddish-brown boulders in the background.

"All aboard," Dad said, making a choo-choo tugging motion with his right arm, ready for a lifetime pass of Disney adventures.

BACKYARD

My favorite part of our family's home was our backyard. It might have seemed like dirt, trees and grass, but ours proved to be so much more. The swimming-pool water glistened under the oak trees, looking its most impeccable just after Mom or Dad skimmed out the leaves with a mesh net attached to a long rod. This was where I became a lifeguard, swimming over to rescue our dog Barkie, who grazed and growled around the pool's perimeter until he fell in the water. His ferocity from a few moments before gave way to a glazed look in his eyes that told me he never had learned to swim.

Each summer, Mom let Robin and me host swimming parties for our friends. We filled an entire table with the tastiest junk foods, sour-cream-flavored potato chips, brownies, sodas and even some healthy carrots that rarely got eaten. We had all sorts of contests to determine who dove off the diving board the best and who could hold her breath the longest underwater. Mom looked out the kitchen window every so often to make sure everyone was still afloat.

When Dad swam with us, we played Marco Polo, a blindfolded game of tag in the pool where one person called out, "Marco," and everyone else responded, "Polo" before scurrying away to escape being tagged. Dad was kind enough to move slowly so that I could reach out and graze his shoulder, and he pretended not to notice when I cheated by opening my eyes.

We finally had to go inside because our fingers looked like prunes. Dad let Robin and me go in first so that we could shower in hot water, just in case the water heater conked out because of all the extra people. He treaded water in the deep end, exercising his leg muscles until Mom peeked her head out the back door and told him it was his turn in the bathroom.

The outdoor cabana next to our pool smelled like musty water, and it was everyone's favorite getaway from the main part of our house. Its walls were whitewashed, and the air conditioner needed an hour's notice to cool the place. Dad brought an old sofa out there, and he liked to read the Sunday paper and fall asleep until one of us kids tapped on the window to pester him or ask him to drive us somewhere. Personally, I enjoyed standing over the sofa and enlarging my eyes until he felt my presence, opened his eyes and jumped up in a startled response to my stare.

The only outdoor restroom was in the cabana, and we were instructed to use it, rather than going in the pool. Once, one of our guests apparently couldn't hold her bladder, and in the middle of our afternoon gathering, everyone noticed a brown trail floating in the deep end of the pool. In that awkward moment, no one wanted to be named the leaky-bladder culprit of the accident.

It was in the backyard that Barkie climbed trees to chase and kill squirrels, which he brought to the back porch like his prized possessions. He leapt in the grass and caught birds in his mouth midair.

From the mounds of dirt near the alley fence, Kristen Bennett and I made mud pies and devised an elaborate system of tunnels centering around the giant castle we formed out of dirt. As a bonus, we added water from the outdoor hose to create a moat and a drawbridge, which fascinated us but turned into a large-scale mess for Mom to clean.

My parents warned us against venturing into the alley, since there might be strangers out there. But as we played, Mom marched fearlessly across the grass holding the trashcan, headed for the dumpster. She unhinged the wooden fence, unloaded the trash, secured the latch and tromped back to the kitchen with the empty trashcan, stopping to stomp the dirt off her feet on the back porch. The whole scenario made Kristen and me feel safe and secure within the boundaries of our fence.

The only time I had to step across the boundary was when Dad and I played kickball. We turned three large stones into bases, and a big clod of dirt served as home base. The more Dad worked with me, the better I got at kicking home runs over the side fence into the Flaglers' backyard. Dad went with me to knock on their door, apologize for the inconvenience and ask to retrieve our rubber ball from their backyard.

There was something magical about our backyard, especially in the summer, when the warm sunshine helped it to come alive, with plenty of help from my friends and family.

MOM'S OUTFITS

In our house, Mom controlled all four wardrobes. Apparently, the tradition dated back to the 70s, when Mom and Dad were newly married, and Mom bought them wild, matching outfits in bold colors. If she wanted to wear one of her multicolor designer dresses, she dressed Dad in a magenta or bright-yellow Polo shirt.

At the time, Dad was in charge of bank deposits for the family furniture business, so he showed up at the clerk's station with large wads of cash from furniture sales. Finally, word circulated back to Dad that the bank tellers were asking around to see if he was an illegal drug dealer, based on the ample chunks of cash and the outrageous outfits. Well, Dad decided he had suffered enough, and he told Mom to tone down his outfits. By the time I was 3, Dad was dressing himself in muted colors like navy and gray, but Mom had stepped up her bold outfits several more notches.

One time, when family friends visited our house, I ran up and hugged George Carrington's tall leg, thinking it was Dad. When I looked up and saw George's smiling face, I ran in embarrassment all the way to the downstairs bathroom, where I locked myself in and planned to cry there all afternoon.

Then, I caught sight of Mom's bright-yellow designer jumpsuit, which hung on the bathroom door like a giant, wearable banana peel. It was made of parachute material and featured all sorts of hidden pockets and zippers, the textile version of a German-fairy-tale castle with trap doors and hidden passages. The sight of it on the hanger captivated little self-pitying me for hours.

Back then, Mom had bright-orange, salon-dyed hair, which she set in rollers that produced curls that swelled like the tide several inches above her head. Combine that with her primary-color eyeshadows, and you can deduce that Mom was quite a sight to behold in our community. You could say she brought the dramatic apparel of the Neiman-Marcus anchor store to our neck of the woods.

When I was about 6, I remember standing with Mom at the Neiman's sunglasses counter in Dallas, where the sales lady handed her pair after pair of the latest, greatest eyewear. That particular fashion season, Oliver Peoples was producing the hottest, most cutting-edge, high-end shades.

As Mom put on a pair of compact, round sunglasses, I looked at her reflection in the small, circular mirror that was secured to the counter. The frames were only slightly larger than her eyeballs. They had a feature where you could flip up the top layer of the metal frames, the part that held the lens.

With these pop-up shades, Mom would have been the perfect backup dancer for MC Hammer's "Too Legit to Quit" music video.

The sales lady looked down at me and said, "Your mom has exquisite taste."

Mom swayed cheerily and asked me, her incredulous child, "So, what do you think?"

I stared at her exposed eyeballs surrounded by the lensless frames. I glanced up at the shaded lens, now extending out past her eyebrows, floating perpendicularly to the rest of the sunglasses. I was honestly trying to help her when I asked, "Are you really going to wear those in public?"

I guess no one appreciated my rhetorical question because Mom not only bought the Oliver Peoples sunglasses but also popped up the movable lens above her eyebrows, MC Hammer-style, the entire time she owned them.

By the time I reached middle school, Mom had moved into the phase of buying matching outfits for herself, Robin and me. The three of us posed for mother-daughter portraits in the backyard, Mom in her head-to-toe floral dress, Robin and I in our calf-length dresses with sailor collars and matching hair bows. We looked ridiculous. It was as if a tornado of bluebonnets had landed on our clothing, sparing only Dad in his navy-blue Adidas tracksuit with white stripes down the sides.

Whenever we would eat out at my dad's favorite cafeteria, Mom, Robin and I led the way to the veggie station, while Dad lingered behind to pile his tray with meat. The cashier needed to know in advance how many trays to put on one ticket, which customers paid on the way out after the meal.

I was the first one to reach the end of the line, so the

cashier, smacking her gum and wearing a hairnet, asked me, "Three trays, miss?"

"No, ma'am, party of four," I said.

She looked at me, then at Mom, then at Robin, all of us outfitted in fields of bluebonnets. Her eyes scanned all the way down the line to Dad in his navy tracksuit.

"That man," she said, pausing, "is with you three?"

"Yes, that's my dad," I said.

Handing me the ticket, the cashier raised one eyebrow as her eyes widened. The four of us marched single file with our cafeteria trays to find a booth. As we passed through the dining room, people rotated their bodies in their booths and tables to stare at our statement-making outfits.

It was like a wedding processional, where guests face the bride until she glides by their pew, at which point they turn again, their eyes following her to the altar. And in that moment, I empathized with caged zoo animals, defenseless but not oblivious to the pointing, slack-jawed onlookers.

"I can't wait to be old enough to pick out my own tracksuits, just like Dad," I grumbled, just above a whisper.

THE FOUR PS

For a number of years, I would only hear of four possibilities for household pets. The choices were puppies, penguins, pandas and pigs, or the four Ps, as my parents nicknamed them.

Why a puppy? Because everyone had a puppy. Really, name one person who didn't have a dog in the family at some point in childhood. In my mind, these statistics made puppies seem less than exotic.

Penguins, however, were exotic, so I wanted one. I could picture one flapping its wings in our backyard and using our swimming pool at its disposal. I imagined we would stare out the window and marvel at its adorableness as our penguin waddled around, trying to run after birds and squirrels.

When I learned that emperor penguins could only survive in Arctic climates, I wanted one even more. With more than 330 days of sunny skies every year, we might not have offered the most ideal climate, but I knew I definitely would be the only kid at Hidden Plains with a pet penguin.

At that point, I decided that I would settle for a panda bear. As an introvert and a vegetarian, I was designed much like a panda bear, which I interpreted as a divine proclamation that I was meant to bring one as my companion to Texas, thus keeping the endangered species alive.

I could envision Ling-Ling or Sing-Sing and myself sitting cross-legged and silent, both of us munching on bamboo chutes in the green space at Shady Oaks Park. I would ask her about rural China and share with her stories of my life in Texas.

The whole time, she would just stare at me, mesmerized, not uttering a peep. My mom would like that because whenever my sister and I squabbled, she sent us to our rooms and told us she didn't want to hear so much as two peeps from either one of us. My preliminary hypothesis was that my panda and I never would argue.

A pig I wanted for noble, humanitarian reasons. My favorite childhood book was *Charlotte's Web* by E.B. White. In it, Fern, a little girl whose father is a farmer, learns that Wilbur, the runt of the baby pigs, will be slaughtered for bacon. Fern then sets out to feed Wilbur from a baby bottle and nurture him back to health in hopes to adopt him as her own.

When I read that, I was convinced that anyone who had ever eaten bacon, sausage, pork or pig in any of its various forms was walking around without a beating heart. If any of my friends or family members dared to order bacon at a restaurant, I blinked at them repeatedly to generate tears, my lower lip trembling, and said a single word, "Wilbur."

Though I may have been out of my league trying to save

all pigs from the omnipotent restaurant industry and my carnivorous peer group, I had to start somewhere by adopting one marvelous pig into the Vaughn family. The future mother in me loved the idea of feeding my Wilbur from a baby bottle and singing him back to health with lullabies in a rocking chair.

After listening to my frantic appeals for one of the four Ps, my parents vetoed all of the above, citing my need to learn small-scale responsibility first by taking care of a simpler pet. And so, weeks later, I was left to interact with the almost-motionless orange goldfish I won at the local fair. It was a dullard of a pet, but I applied my best efforts toward talking to it and keeping its vital signs going. It was my only shot at someday playing mommy to either a puppy, penguin, panda or pig, whichever one my parents preferred.

KRISTEN BENNETT

Kristen Bennett and I first met when my sister Robin and I were walking our baby dolls in their strollers down 8th Street. Mom would only let us go to the end of the block, and the corner house near Shady Oaks Park happened to be where the Bennetts had just moved.

Barefoot on her front porch stood 3-year-old Kristen, a wisp of a girl with white-blonde hair pulled into a side ponytail. I couldn't see that her two front teeth were missing, but I could see the giant, multicolor hair bow stuck to the right side of her head. Her ponytail wiggled as she waved fervently to Robin and me. Instinctively, I knew I had found my best friend.

Robin and I hurried home, no longer concerned with our make-believe children. I tugged at Mom's pant leg, begging her to let me play with Kristen. Mom wanted to meet Kristen's parents first, so our neighbor Jackie Henderson, only one year older than me, said, "I can arrange that."

She got the idea for my whole family show up at the Bennetts' door on Halloween to trick or treat. That way, Dad and Mom could meet Dave and Sue without seeming skeptical. As it turned out, they approved, and so began our lifelong friendship.

Kristen and I attended Hidden Plains Presbyterian School together from preschool through ninth grade. Life was good with Kristen by my side. After school, we borrowed Sue's floral dresses and high heels, our tiny figures barely filling out a third of outfits designed for a grown woman. With our hair in pigtails, we kicked off our gaping shoes and tripped over Sue's long dresses trying to catch butterflies with our hands at the park.

In the summer, we had pool parties in Kristen's backyard. Recreating the Olympic games, we rated each other's dives off the diving board and invented a game called "Surfin' USA." The goal of the game was to remain standing on top of a plastic pool raft as we balanced on our flimsy "surfboards" and belted out The Beach Boys' lyrics we had memorized from our parents' albums. The surfer girl who crashed into the water first had to pronounce her opponent the winner.

By that time, Sue was back from the grocery store, and when we saw her rush from the garage to the back door with two brown paper sacks, that was our cue to get out of the water. After all, we had sent her off with special requests of cherry popsicles for me and chocolate popsicles for Kristen. We followed Sue into the kitchen, where we ate our popsicles, soaking wet, dripping chlorinated water all over the floor.

In the Bennetts' den, we choreographed our own dance

videos to songs like the Spice Girls' "Spice Up Your Life" and Cyndi Lauper's "Girls Just Want To Have Fun." We persuaded one of our moms to film our moves on her camcorder so that we could watch and critique our performances on the small screen.

Kristen and I founded businesses together in the cabana near my family's backyard pool, and after much debate we agreed on the incorporated name of Veronica Leslie KrAsh. Kristen chose Veronica, since it was her favorite girl's name, and I chose Leslie because that was my favorite. We compromised on the last name, KrAsh, by combining our two first names. Together, we launched countless entrepreneurial endeavors as the owners of restaurants, schools and lemonade stands. Our parents were our best customers, and it cost them a pretty penny to shop at our establishments, even though they paid the rent too.

Kristen and I were merciless to our babysitters. Right before Brooke Sparks, a high-school student, came to keep us, the two of us concocted a plan to dress me in a ski mask and ski goggles, both items pulled tightly over my face, in order to convince Brooke that I was a blind-and-deaf foreign exchange student.

But there was a catch. Kristen told Brooke that Kristen and I could communicate through an audible language only we could understand. The effect sounded like distressed dolphins yelping for human assistance. All went well until Kristen threw Gak, a slimy, green blob of goo, onto the ceiling. My eyes darted up and then plunged downward as the Gak hit the floor.

"I thought she couldn't see anything," Brooke said, and we knew she was on to us. In our finest attempt at acting, we had at least entertained ourselves.

Later in the evening, Kristen and I hosted messy parades in the hallway, throwing fists full of colorful confetti into the air. We skipped over the pieces, screaming with glee, jamming tiny confetti particles into the carpet's crevices. When it was time to clean up, Kristen and I went missing from the scene. We climbed to the top shelf of the hallway closet and hid together in that tiny space until Brooke found us an hour or two later.

"Our other babysitters cleaned up after the last parade," we explained to Brooke, pointing her to the whereabouts of Sue's handheld vacuum. Was it any wonder no one wanted to babysit us twice?

I always thought of Kristen as family, close enough to be a sister. In fact, we were sisters when we played "Courage Mountain," a game we invented after seeing a movie by the same name about an orphan who survived a winter in the Swiss Alps.

The life experiences of the film's plucky heroine seemed altogether enviable on the big screen, so by imagination only, Kristen and I became orphans who wrapped our bodies in woven afghans for warmth and protection from the blustery Alpine wind and snow. Onward we plodded, scaling the sofas and love seats in my parents' den as if they were the rocky slopes of a mountain range.

Occasionally, we were swept away by a pretend blustery norther, prompting us to dispense our "medicine," which was a spoonful each of Smarties candy. We carefully unwrapped the plastic coating so as not to forfeit any of our self-prescribed antidote, which would dissolve in the snow.

Kristen understood my fears, even the ones I didn't want her to know. During middle school, we watched way too many true-crime television shows that reenacted crimes to catch culprits still on the loose. After each segment, I convinced myself that the national felons all had found their way to our neighborhood. It's safe to say that I worked myself into a state of paranoia about a potential kidnapping. As a result of that fear, I would ask my mom to drive me to Kristen's house at the end of the block.

"Why don't you just walk?" Mom asked, totally unaware of my mind's inner workings. So I did, except I ran, whirling my head to the side to make sure no one was following me. Kristen knew what was going on, but I denied it.

Then one day a car was driving slowly next to me, and I saw that the driver was looking at a sheet of paper and then squinting my way. I could see Kristen outside on her front porch, and I knew if I could survive this maniacal abductor, I could convince Mom to drive me to Kristen's house from then on.

I sprinted down the street, not stopping until I had slammed Kristen's front door behind me. Kristen burst out laughing.

"Ashley's afraid of the pizza man," she said.

She repeated the phrase over and over, pausing only to contain her outbursts of laughter. Sure enough, a high-school boy in a baseball hat, confused about whether he had shown up at the right house, delivered two pepperoni pizzas to Kristen's house, courtesy of Sue.

Back then, Sue and Mom were caught up in the Jane Fonda and Richard Simmons workout-video craze. Kristen and I scarfed down our pizzas and then "sweated to the oldies" alongside our moms. The four of us emulated Richard Simmons' movements on the TV screen, all of us dressed in our spandex leotards and tights. Wherever we went, Kristen and

I ran, skipped, jumped or bounced, and so we both remained stick thin throughout our childhoods.

Sue and Mom wanted to ensure our summers were brimming with activities.

They signed us up for a basketball camp at a local high school, but we countered that we weren't interested. As a final compromise, they bribed us.

The four of us struck a deal that Kristen and I would attend the morning drill sessions if Mom and Sue would let us do something fun, our choice of course, every afternoon. While the other female campers did right-handed layups and ran sprints, Kristen and I bounced our basketballs in the corner, discussing whether we'd rather play miniature golf or hit the wave pool at our local water park.

At age 12, Kristen and I reached the pinnacle of our tomboy phase, and our dads jumped at the chance to take us fishing in Arkansas. Dave owned a used-car dealership, and he always secured the most unusual contraptions to drive. For this trip, he brought home an oversized, industrial van. He and Dad sat in the modest front cabin, blaring political talk shows and discussing their viewpoints at the top of their lungs.

Kristen and I sectioned off the rear cabin by folding down the back seat, which opened up twice as much space for us. We spread quilts on the floor and opened paper sacks filled with enough food to survive the biblical flood. Our CD players repeated the same song, Lisa Loeb's "Stay." Once we arrived at our campsite in Arkansas, Kristen and I relished the simple life, including the adventure of trudging to the outhouse in the middle of the night.

At home and at school, Kristen and I were inseparable. We endured off-season basketball practice for students who chose not to play tennis. There were only three of us in the class, Elise Rousseau, Kristen and me, and Coach Chalmers ran us until we took turns running to the bathroom to throw up. It bonded us for life.

Coach Chalmers was trying to prepare us for basketball season. He wanted us to stay in shape since Coach Hobbs' practices were equally as grueling. Mom empathized with our suffering, so she took us to the drive thru of an Italian fast-food restaurant as an after-school treat. By the time we made it to basketball season, we were full of baked ziti and breadsticks, even more out of shape than before.

Kristen and I knew each other's quirks, and we even had our own lingo. We created the word "schwa" to refer to the cowlicks that formed in my hair after a long night of sleeping on one side.

Once, I mentioned to her that I never shaved the back of my legs because they just weren't that hairy. She wrinkled her face. "Even so, that's pretty gross," she said. "I wouldn't repeat that to anyone else."

I liked to tease Kristen about the grammatical mistakes she made during middle school, like saying, "amen't I?" instead of "aren't I," as in, "Amen't I spending the night at your house tonight?" To this day, she's the only person I've ever known who calls her morning meal "breakthest" instead of "breakfast."

Only Kristen knew about the incident when we buried her dead hamster in a cardboard box, vowing to dig him up 20 years later as part of our time-capsule experiment. We couldn't wait a full week before resurfacing the box with a shovel. Kristen and I were so horrified by his appearance that we made a pact never to tell anyone else what we had done.

Then there was the time we ate chicken noodle soup at

Kristen's house. Prone to choking, I swallowed one of the extra-long noodles down the wrong tube, and Kristen waited patiently while I coughed up enough of the noodle to pull out the remainder from my throat.

"That was a long one. It just kept coming," she said with the empathy only a best friend could impart. It was disgusting, and I was so grateful that it was Kristen who sat across from me, straight-faced, realizing there was nothing she could do but offer her unconditional support.

There were other not-so-good times, like the time in Kristen's treehouse when I pulled my sister Robin's braid. Dave corrected me, and I took it out on Kristen.

"I'm going home, and we're never going to be friends again," I said, storming out of the treehouse. It wasn't the last time I used immature tactics to make Kristen suffer.

I cherished every moment of play time to the degree that when she told me she had to go home, I said in a huff, "Fine, I was just about to fix some brownie sundaes with bananas and whip cream, but since you have to go, well that's too bad."

Moments like these are safely stored in the annals of our 30-year friendship, and they make up only a snapshot of the countless memories we've shared.

THE MOUSE TRAP

The highlight of my weekends was hosting my friends at our house for rollerblading. My dad had taken me to the mall weeks earlier to buy my first pair of skates at Champs Sports. They couldn't be just any skates, though. They had to be brand-name, state-of-the-art Rollerblades.

I prided myself on buying a pair with only one brake, which was attached to the back end of the right skate. I wasn't convinced I needed brakes at all, but all of the adults at the sporting-goods store, including the sales clerk and my dad, advised me otherwise.

"Fall, how could I fall?" I reasoned. Outfit me with a headband, some kneepads and a few temporary tattoos, and I could probably land an endorsement deal in California.

"I know you're a good skater," Dad said, "but it's good to have at least one way to stop, just in case you fall."

I smiled sweetly at him, listening to the echoes of the major laughter inside my head.

Mom said I could invite Julia Poppy over the next day to skate. I had already planned to give her the right skate, the one with the brake, since obviously she wasn't as experienced as I was in wheelies and death-defying jumps inches off the concrete.

All afternoon we whirled through the neighborhood, undaunted by the cars, speed bumps and sidewalk-hogging dogs that attempted to slow our pace. When we finally needed a break, we spanned the long stretch of sidewalk that led to our garage. Our skates stayed on as we raced into the kitchen for a snack. Food crumbs trailed our path to the den. Mom recently had torn out the carpet in the den in favor of the red brick underneath, and I could just kiss her for it.

With newfound energy, Julia and I had no need for rest. We blared music from the stereo and conducted a disco party, skating in circles around the room. The two of us formed a disco chain, Julia's hands fastened to my hips.

Leading the way, my arms were unattached, so I did the coolest disco move, modeled to me by John Travolta in *Saturday Night Fever.* My right arm did the diagonal disco, moving in the air from top right to bottom left, index finger pointed and all. With no warning whatsoever, Julia screamed, clutching my waist with the voracity of a blood pressure cuff.

"What is it, what's wrong?" I asked, my head whipping backward to identify the commotion. The sharp angle sent my brakeless rollerblade skidding forward in one giant swoop. My rear hit the ground when the image of Dad, saying jovially at the sporting store, "just in case you fall," replayed in my mind.

But that was nothing compared to the rude awakening of

opening my eyes, now at ground level. I was face to face with two baby mice, their bottom halves stuck to the glue trap that was securely fastened to Julia's brake. They were alive, and I don't know who squealed louder, them or me. I scrambled to jump to my feet, so nervous I kept tumbling down, creating the blueprint for two knees full of soon-to-be bruises.

My next thought was that the parents of these baby mice could be on the loose. A couple of days before, I had been sitting on the sofa eating my dinner when I thought I saw something dark and small scamper from behind the television to the kitchen. Well, the mystery was solved. Two down, but who knew how many cousin-and-uncle rodents inhabited our home.

I hightailed it in the opposite direction from Julia and hopped onto our leather sofa for shelter. She had been a petrified statue up to that point, but then Julia dragged her skate and its unwelcome guests toward me.

"Nooooooo! Stay away," I bellowed, shielding myself by throwing pillows at her. Julia was my good friend, but when it came to irrational fears, it was survival of the fittest. Then, I did what any kid or grown up would do.

"Mommmmmmm," I screamed, hoping the sound would reach the far corners of whatever room she was in at that moment. Moms have a sixth sense for these emergency situations. She flew threw several rooms, and I felt relieved by her rushing to my defense. But her eyes went to Julia.

"Oh no, you poor thing," she said. I was horrified by what she did next.

My own flesh and blood sat on the brick floor and, with bare hands, tugged on the mouse pad until the glue loosened off Julia's skate. Our background noise consisted of constant, shrill rodent chatter. I had a series of flashbacks while I watched in disgust.

Robin's dog Barkie was infamous for jumping in the air and catching birds in his mouth. He also climbed trees, outwitting squirrels and bringing them dead to our back door. Unfazed, Mom picked up the birds and squirrels by their tails, plopped them in a brown paper sack and vanished to the dumpster. I chided Mom from the safety of the kitchen, hollering out the window, "You can get diseases from doing that kind of stuff." Mom really needed help, and plastic gloves.

They say it's hard for people to change, and for Mom that was true. Throughout the weeks after Barkie's exploits and our house guests the mice, she continued brown-bagging animals to the dumpster.

But I changed. Truly I did. Before, I had been lax about safety precautions, but not anymore. I stopped walking around the house barefoot. I quit eating dinner on the den floor. No longer did I stretch out beside the TV, doing tens of dozens of sit-ups with my face sharing the same stomping ground as these would-be trespassers.

I avoided Barkie as best I could, but when I did go near him, I wore mittens, just in case the dead animals he toted by mouth had transferred some communicable disease. I even apologized to Julia, telling her I was sorry for ditching my fallen comrade in favor of the fetal position on the sofa.

"It's okay," she said, smiling. "I've been practicing my skating. Next time I come over, if you still have mice, you get to wear the skate with the brake."

Later that winter, Mom discovered steel wool. She singlehandedly located and plugged every hole in the kitchen wall where the mice were entering. Our house had become a top tourist destination for either freeloading or deceased animals. No longer would mice nosh on our food crumbs and squeak at our human guests. Thanks to Mom, we had officially closed our doors for the season.

Yes, I had given her adolescent attitude, but I was so grateful for Mom's heroism and toughness. She never shied away from a challenge, be it living, be it bloody, be it decaying, that no one else wanted to face.

BRANDON PRESCOTT II

Brandon Prescott II was one of those boys in class who balanced out the perfectionist girls. Teachers spent as much time managing Brandon's havoc as they did teaching us our daily lesson. His assigned seat was on the back row in the seat closest to the exit door. Consider it the easiest point of access to the principal's office.

Annette Prescott, Brandon's mom, was one of my mom's best friends, so Mom was aware of his antics from the time he was born. When Brandon II was 5, his parents, Brandon I and Annette, enrolled their son in pre-first, an outlet for kids who weren't quite ready for first grade.

At the end of every school year, teachers practically danced down the halls as they escorted Brandon, pulling him by the top of his Hidden Plains sweater, to meet his new teacher. The teacher bent down to extend her hand to Brandon, who slapped it with a high five before breezing past her to survey the classroom he would destroy the following school year.

During our preschool years, Mom volunteered at the Hidden Plains library. She led story time, and each week she carefully selected a book to read to an audience of tiny 4-year-olds. There we sat, cross-legged on the plastic mat, quietly waiting for Mom's soothing voice to entertain us as she created distinctive voices and expressions for each character.

By that time, Brandon was long gone. He hid behind the shelves entitled "Mystery" and dog-eared the pages of *The Boxcar Children* series. Then he began interchanging the alphabetical order of books, mixing E.B. White's writings with those of authors whose last names started with "A." Before he could tamper with the Dewey Decimal catalog in the corner, Mom noticed him in her peripheral vision.

Calmly and confidently, she inserted his name into the story. One story happened to be the tall tale of Paul Bunyan, the adventurous lumberjack depicted as a giant. Brandon's ears perked up when he heard the part about getting to carry an ax and travel with his animal companion, Babe the Blue Ox. Entranced, he rejoined us on the mat and listened as Mom dialogued using the manliest, burliest Bunyan voice she could muster.

Years passed, and though times had changed, Brandon had not. At age 12, he slugged Mr. Cullen, his piano teacher, in the ribcage for encouraging Brandon to practice at home. Annette begged some random, amateur piano teacher on the other side of town to accept him as a student.

That new venture didn't last long. Five minutes with Brandon, and Mr. Lee called Annette at home to pick up Brandon immediately. Right before he left, Brandon ran over to the Yamaha keyboard, tickling the ivories or rather slamming his fists on the keys in defiance. And with that, he cued his exit out the screen door.

That same year, my dad volunteered to teach Sunday school at our church, Hidden Plains Baptist. Though I was a year younger than Brandon, he had attended pre-first, so now we were in the same grade both at Hidden Plains and at church.

Each week, our class sectioned off into small groups to discuss this week's Bible lesson. Boys were in one room, girls in another. Apparently, it was Dad's turn to wrangle Brandon because he was assigned to lead the boys.

The next thing I knew, there was a commotion, and the head teacher was using all of his might to lead Brandon out of the classroom. It was a struggle, since Brandon disputed his expulsion by employing his whole body as dead weight. The more Brandon resisted, the more the teacher's face reddened and blued and purpled, until finally he collapsed from exhaustion.

His wife walked briskly out of the room and returned 10 minutes later with Annette. Apparently, she had to walk behind the pulpit during Dr. O'Leary's sermon to locate Annette, who sang in the Hidden Plains Baptist choir. Still dressed in her long, burgundy robe with a waist-length, white overlay, Annette marched into the room, scanning it for the poster boy of disorderly conduct.

The usual suspect, who just moments before was darting around the room, tossing his head back as he screamed, "Order in the court, order in the court," became as quiet as a church mouse when he saw his mom.

I'll never forget what Annette did next. She lifted the long sleeves of her choir robe up to her elbows, dropped her knees to the floor and hoisted her 12-year-old son over her shoulder. The blue hymnal she was carrying hit the ground with a thud.

As they left, she turned to my dad and said, "I'm so sorry that Brandon punched you in the stomach. Please find it in your heart to forgive him in the next decade or two." Annette swooped around to walk out of the room. Brandon, still on her back, was now face forward with his teachers and classmates.

"He deserved it," Brandon said. "He asked me all the hard questions."

Brandon stuck out his tongue at Dad, a gesture he considered safe because Annette couldn't see it. Dad took it in stride, laughing about the incident when he recounted it to Mom.

"I asked Brandon the tough ones because he's the smartest boy in the class," Dad said, shrugging his shoulders. "Kid's got potential," he continued. "It'll be interesting to see if he ends up in the Oval Office or in trouble all the time."

For years, the latter hypothesis seemed more probable. Our Hidden Plains headmaster, Dr. Champion, had written a book about his job as head of operations at the Olympics. A copy of it sat on the coffee table near Dr. C's office. One of its main functions was to serve as reading material for unruly students who awaited their fate with Dr. C, our kind leader who had high expectations for his students. Brandon visited the principal's office so frequently during middle school that he could quote entire passages from that book.

But Dr. C had an eye on Brandon, recognizing the promising future within his grasp. The charismatic headmaster parlayed the wisdom he had acquired as a former presidential advisor into educational orations directed at Brandon. Then, after their hour-long sessions, Brandon returned to class, where he shot spit wads into Amy Johansson's long, flowing hair, a target so thick that Amy was totally unaware of what was happening.

And so it was back to the daily do-si-do, swinging through the doors of the principal's office to see Dr. C. and then back through the doors of English class to be scolded by Mrs Graham.

It was a running joke, until the day it became personal to me. Since my last name began with "V," my seat in English class was next to Brandon's, two seats from the classroom door at the back of the room. The seating chart was alphabetical, except for Brandon, who was the exception to every rule.

There I was, focused and taking notes on Mrs. Graham's explanation of the usage of "your and you're" and "their, there and they're," when Brandon leaned toward my desk and asked, "Think we'll ever need to know this stuff in the real world? I sure don't." Problem was, when he uttered the "sh" sound, his gum, which was prohibited at Hidden Plains, flew out of his mouth and into my hair, not the bottom portion of my long hair, but right smack in the middle of it.

Mrs. Graham postponed the lesson, and she replaced Brandon in the desk next to mine as she utilized every effort--her fingers, a pencil eraser and finally a piece of Laffy Taffy--to unstick the gum from my hair. Nothing worked, and I erupted in tears when she approached me with a pair of scissors.

All of my classmates shared the four desks adjacent to mine, occupying the chairs, table tops and the floor for front-row seats to the shearing. Brandon stood behind my chair, placing his hands on my shoulders in an ill-received attempt to console me.

"I'm crying with ya, babe," he said as Mrs. Graham chopped off entire sections of my hair. I responded with a gasp, my tears so heavy that I choked out an inadvertent snort. No, buddy, you're not crying with me, I thought. Losing your hair against your will is something you just don't understand. Incidentally, decades later, Brandon's hairline started receding, and he did understand.

I'd like to think that I played a minor role in Brandon's transformation, though no one is entirely sure how or when it happened. In eighth grade, Brandon organized an event at Hidden Plains called, "See You at the Pole," which marked a day of prayer at schools across the nation.

He settled down at age 19, marrying a lovely girl named Caroline. By his late 20s, Brandon was a college-educated father of three little girls. He had worked for a technology startup in San Francisco and then earned an MBA from Stanford. When our paths crossed again, he was in the process of starting his own company.

Brandon and Caroline invited me to their home for dinner. We had lasagna, and I got acquainted with his daughters. Christina, sweet, reserved and polite, was about 5 years old. She poked me during my pre-dinner conversation with the family and said, "Excuse me, hands in your lap at the table."

Her parents, horrified, said, "Christina, Miss Ashley is our guest, and she's an adult." They told me they were using my visit as an opportunity to teach their girls etiquette. Claire, the baby, was a little bundle of joy. Caroline had to rush her to the emergency clinic after dinner for an unexpected minor infection, but precious Claire never cried or lost her joy.

Emily, the middle child, was about 2. She had a constant look of mischief in her twinkling eyes. She stood in her chair at the dinner table, twirling around in circles, saying, "Ta da," entertaining us all. Brandon, with a laid-back approach to parenting, was now the most mellow, mature male I'd ever met.

"Emily, we don't scoot back in our chair," he instructed. "Emily, we don't spit our food, we eat it." When she ran from the table and punctured the mini blinds, he said, "Ouch, that's going to come out of our deposit. Can you say deposit?"

"Deposit," Emily said.

We went outside to play, and Emily begged me to swing her in the air by her arms. She sprinted back and forth from a tree to the adults, slapping our hands breathlessly each time she passed by. She climbed the wall that separated us from the busy street before her dad corrected her gently. He tried to think of energy-draining games for her to play.

"Anything to exhaust some of her energy before bedtime," he said to Caroline and me. I could imagine that putting this spark plug to bed at night required at least as much patience and commitment as starting his business from scratch.

"Emily's the most like you as a kid, isn't she?" I asked.

"Yep," he said.

And we both laughed a nervous, ironic laugh, knowing Brandon would have years, make that decades, of raising a daintier, yet equally as unruly version of himself.

THE SPELLING BEE

The annual Hidden Plains Spelling Bee was fast approaching. Normally, I was not a competitive person, especially in terms of basketball games. Dad had offered for years to pay me for each foul I committed. His attempt to elicit any sort of enthusiasm or aggressiveness on the court had failed miserably.

Academic contests, however, were a different matter. Winning the spelling bee led to a path of success, of this I was certain. Memorizing challenging words would skyrocket my SAT scores, boosting my chances of admission to an Ivy League school, which, I figured, would slingshot me straight to a successful jaunt in life.

Of course, the more immediate reward would be an all-expenses-paid trip to the National Spelling Bee in Washington, D.C. The stakes were high, and I was in it to win it. No word was off limits, and I'd face some fierce competition.

The Cannes brothers, Mark and Clark Cannes, were last year's first-and-second-place winners. Their early exposure to linguistics, Exhibit A being their rhyming names given at birth, would foreshadow their lifelong prowess in Math Team, Odyssey of the Mind, Mensa and, yes, the Hidden Plains Spelling Bee. They were twin-boy brainiacs one grade below mine whose Friday and Saturday evenings consisted of, you guessed it, practicing for the annual spelling bee.

After last year's victory, the headline in our school newspaper read, "The Cannes Brothers Cannes Spell." Unfortunately, the writer of that headline could not.

My pre-bee stress began early that year, so Mom and Dad helped me study. During dinner, they quizzed me on miscellaneous words like precipice, cantankerous, uranium and onomatopoeia, the brainteasing word that imitates a sound. This year, I would have to reach the summit of academia to beat the Cannes brothers.

I did mental calisthenics throughout the day, carrying around 3x5-inch index cards featuring problematic words. I crafted unique sentences, spelling in my mind any multisyllabic words.

"Indeed, I would love it if Coach Hobbs would abdicate his throne and retire from coaching basketball. Abdicate. A-B-D-I-C-A-T-E. Abdicate." My antics kept me entertained all day.

But then I saw with my own eyes that Kevin Whitley was practicing too. Kevin had earned the reputation as a mama's boy because every day Marianne Whitley sashayed into the school cafeteria, where together she and her son ate takeout during the lunch hour. Pen to paper, I calculated that Kevin was getting 45 extra minutes of parental vocabulary building, approximately 900 words per day more than me. This curveball upped the ante, and I was chomping at the bit to mentally foul my unexpected opponent. I wondered if Dad would follow up on his offer to pay me.

Kevin practiced for the contest everywhere, even in history class with Mr. Llewellyn, this year's spelling-bee judge.

"Ahhh, Mr. Whitley, would you please disseminate these graded papers to your classmates?" Mr. Llewellyn asked.

"Sir, could you give me the definition and the origin of that word? I'm not familiar," Kevin said.

"Ahhh, beg your pardon?" Mr. Llewellyn asked.

"It's one of the rules of the spelling bee," Kevin said. "I'm allowed to ask for the definition and etymological root of the word."

"Ahhhh, Mr. Whitley, this is not the spelling bee. This is American history class so, uh, behave, uh, okay?" Mr. Llewellyn said. Every word Mr. Llewellyn said sounded like it was funneled through a foghorn.

"Yes, sir, but I'm just exercising my rights as a spelling-bee contestant," Kevin said. Under his breath, he muttered, "I'm also allowed to ask for an example in a sentence."

We had flexed our mental muscles long enough. The day of the spelling bee was upon us. About a hundred entrants filed into the gymnasium, glancing through our flashcards one final time before tossing them into the trashcan. They now were contraband, an immediate disqualification if found anywhere near the rows of chairs assembled along the gymnasium stage.

Already, I was nervous, but when I spotted the number of movie cameras, the faces of Hidden Plains parents partially visible behind them, in the audience rows, I knew the marathon of perspiration running under my armpits had begun.

Round one was underway. One by one, the judges hit the

buzzer on my classmates, eliminated on words like fissiparous, smorgasbord and cirrhosis. The Cannes brothers sailed through on engineering-and-medical words, which happened to be their speciality.

Kevin Whitley cleared as well, nailing the word "paupiette," a thin slice of meat or fish wrapped around a filling. Who knew? I sure didn't. Kevin had proven to be a formidable opponent. He stared at me as he returned to his seat. I could read his lips.

"Just warming up," he mouthed.

My word was "soliloquy." I remembered it from one of my evening practice sessions with Dad. He had given the example that I delivered a soliloquy to him and Mom, citing the reasons I wanted a dog. I moved on to the next round, a small victory.

It was round two, and Mark Cannes was up.

"Your word is ally," Mr. Llewellyn said. But with his nasal intonation, the pronunciation came out as "a lie."

Either overconfident or too proud, Mark didn't ask him use it in a sentence. "Ally," Mark said. "A-L-I-E. Ally."

"I'm sorry, Mr. Cannes," Mr. Llewellyn said. "That is incorrect." Mark's head dropped, and he walked despondently off the stage.

His brother's seemingly impossible misstep must have thrown Clark Cannes off his game. He butchered "gegenschein," a softball word for the scientific Cannes twins.

What was happening? Mark Cannes eliminated on a disyllabic no-brainer?

Clark Cannes caught up on a trisyllabic word in his area of expertise? Many parents wore frozen expressions. Perhaps they were thinking, "Had the twins not eaten their alphabet

Cheerios? Had they imbibed something toxic from the water fountain?"

Kevin Whitley approached the platform. "Ahhh, your word is essay," Mr. Llewellyn said. Kevin thought for a moment.

"Essay," Kevin repeated aloud. "Essay...essay." Several seconds of silence followed.

"Yes, Mr. Whitley, your word is essay," Mr. Llewellyn said.

Kevin gave him a befuddled look. "Essay...essay...essay," Kevin said. Why was Kevin repeating the word over and over, I wondered. He knew he was supposed to say the word, spell it and say it again.

"Would you like the origin of the word, Mr. Whitley?" Mr. Llewellyn asked.

Judges weren't supposed to extend such an offer, but Hidden Plains authority figures erred on the side of leniency.

"Umm, okay," Kevin said, more perplexed than ever.

"Essay, 1590s, a short, nonfiction literary composition. The word is from the Latin 'exigere,' to test out," Mr. Llewellyn said.

"Essay...S-A...essay," Kevin said.

All that had just happened suddenly clicked inside my head. The silence continued. Kristen Bennett yawned.

"Uh, Mr. Whitley, if you don't spell the word, we'll have to disqualify you. There's a strict time limit, uhhh okay?" Mr. Llewellyn said.

I was getting uncomfortable. The Nina, Pinta and Santa Maria could have launched from my sweat-drenched armpits. I felt Kevin's pain, and when I'd heard enough, I sprang to my feet.

"Mr. Llewellyn, don't you understand?" I pleaded. "Kevin is trying to spell the word. He thinks 'essay' is spelled 's' period 'a' period. That's why he keeps repeating it over and over. He doesn't know how to spell the word 'essay,' okay?" I had a habit of transferring other people's humiliating situations onto myself.

And with that, I ran off behind the curtains, an automatic forfeiture of the Hidden Plains Spelling Bee title. The stage of contestants was empty, and no one cheered. Parents ejected the cassette tapes from their cameras, discarding them in the bins outside the gymnasium.

The year 1995 would forever be known among Hidden Plains alumni as the only time in history when every candidate was disqualified from the annual spelling bee. That year, there would be no trophy presentation, no bragging rights, no resume padding, no trip to Washington, D.C. and, most notably, no ridiculous headline in the next day's school newspaper.

And that, my friends, was the one thing we all could celebrate.

MRS. HENSLEY

During my middle-school years, school children in Texas spent an entire chunk of the day focusing on the history of our state. Mrs. Linda Hensley taught sixth-grade Texas history at Hidden Plains. There, in a compact classroom, she told her students, many of us seventh-generation Texans, stories about our ancestors. We learned about the Texas Revolution, where ordinary citizens battled for our land and our honor at the Alamo.

"William B. Travis drew a line in the sand, asking those to step forth who would rather die than surrender to General Santa Ana," Mrs Hensley said. "Students, all but one person took that step."

Then she proclaimed a phrase that would become mine and my classmates' battle cry. "Remember the Alamo!" she said, thrusting her fist high, reminding us that those who had died for the Republic of Texas uttered those very same words.

As descendants of people who had formed the only sovereign republic in the Union, we were instructed by Mrs. Hensley to challenge authority figures and defend our beliefs to the death. In short, we were made to be different. And Mrs. Hensley was made to be different too.

Her hair fell just below the chin but seemed shorter due to frequent perms, which created tight, frizzy tendrils, many of them clipped to the side with bobby pins. She wore large-rimmed, masculine glasses with tiny, bifocal lenses in the bottom center. With her right index finger, she slid her glasses up and down the length of her nose, depending on whether she was looking at her students or the fine print in the history textbook. She did this with such frequency that the motion looked like eager children repeatedly climbing up and cascading down a playground slide.

Mrs. Hensley's defining characteristic was her distinctive wardrobe. During the 1990s, adults, especially teachers, were batty about two-piece pantsuits. Looking back, I can't decipher whether I learned more about Texas history from my lengthy homework assignments or from Mrs. Hensley's demonstrative outfits. Her long-sleeved cotton shirts featured the same patterns over and over, as did the attached, matching pants.

Mrs. Hensley was a tall woman with a boxy shape, which gave the outfits plenty of room to serve as a montage of our state's various landscapes. One pantsuit in particular was primarily navy blue with green, white and brown as accent colors.

The print seemed to be a documentation of the popular 1960s game Cowboys and Indians. In one corner, the left side of Mrs. Hensley's blouse, we had the gun-wielding cowboys with their covered wagons and their prickly cacti. In the other corner, the right side of her blouse, we had the Indians, with their painted teepees and their archery weapons aimed at the cowboys.

It wouldn't have been so distracting, except that the same pattern spawned varying reproductions of itself from Mrs. Hensley's neck to her ankles. The only break in pattern came from the wobbly pouch, what we called her "teacher gut," which protruded below the brown, woven belt fastened high above her hips.

When Reagan Ingram asked her why there were so many Indians and teepees on her outfit, Mrs. Hensley responded by giving us a brief history lesson on Cherokee, Choctaw and Chippewa culture, including their use of every part of the buffalo for food and shelter. They would hereby be referred to as Native Americans, not Indians, Mrs. Hensley mandated.

"Native Americans inhabited our country before the explorers arrived," she said. "Indians are from India."

Something about the way Mrs. Hensley dressed clued us in that she would be an easy target for our immature antics. Also, the seventh-grade class told us so. Mrs. Hensley was the quintessential school-trip sponsor. She signed up to chaperone everything, which gave her a flunking coolness grade among her students. Seeing our history teacher wear night cream and pajama pants in the adjoining bunk bed was not on our list of beloved pastimes.

Word was the grade ahead of us had made her cry during their class trip by using the host site's entire stock of toilet paper to wrap the trees and buildings. Also, someone's lunch tray ended up through the dining-room window, and vandalism didn't exactly jibe with the Hidden Plains mission. The administration punished our class by eliminating our annual trip. Instead of holding a grudge against the rowdy seventh graders, we held it against Mrs. Hensley and committed boisterous acts of rebellion in her classroom.

Mrs. Hensley always kept a can of diet soda on her desk. When she turned to face the chalkboard, Holly Gallagher tiptoed to her desk, placing a stick of Scotch tape over the opening of her soda. The next time Mrs. Hensley reached for her drink, liquid was scarce, causing her to arch her head way back. Soda came gushing out onto her face and clothes, even into her nostrils. Then Brandon Prescott II put a giant stapler to her booklets of sticky notes, rendering one of her favorite teacher's aids useless.

I admit with regret that the all-time low of our scheming was the deaf trick. Yes, we tried, with initial success I might add, to convince Mrs. Hensley that she had suddenly and permanently lost her hearing.

At the beginning of class, we sat at our desks and, like mimes, mouthed words to each other, moving our arms and making noiseless motions. We planned carefully in advance, turning the classroom television on but adjusting the volume to mute.

Mrs. Hensley never had heard the sound of silence in her classroom. She poked around inside her ears and flicked her eardrums to see if they were working properly. She ran over to the classroom door, which was open, and released the doorstop.

The door slammed shut, and her panicky expression morphed instantly into one of relief, then indignation.

We erupted into laughter, running around the room screaming, "Remember the Alamo," our battle cry as we pelted paper clips at her and each other. She waved her instructional stick, normally used to point to items on the chalkboard during lectures, at each of us as if it would activate a magic teacher wand that would calm our hyper behavior.

Finally, she offered to let us watch a film during class, albeit an educational one highlighting life and culture on a Native American reservation. It became evident that she had not screened the film in advance because a topless Native American woman approached the camera in quizzical fascination. The boys' jaws dropped.

"Good choice," Brandon said.

Mrs. Hensley darted in front of the television in terror. That day, she had opted to wear a long skirt. Pinching together her thumbs and index fingers, she held both sides of her skirt at shoulder height to cover the nudity that Reagan, Brandon and the other boys surely would report home to their mothers. But her body faced the students, not the TV, and surprisingly, the fullness of her skirt could not blanket the entire screen.

"I can still see the native woman's boobs," Reagan said.

There was nothing she could do but go into the hall and "have a moment." When she returned, she wiped her eyes discretely, tossing a used tissue into the trash.

It's hard to believe that Mrs. Hensley invited us to her family's ranch after these incidents, which lived on when Reagan and Brandon threatened to unleash spray paint and silly string on her homestead.

As adults, we saw the light about the way we treated her, but back then, this was the stuff dreams were made of. After all, she had broken the cardinal rude of Teacher 101--do not let let your sugar-crazed students take control of the classroom.

Our excuse? It was in our blood. We were Texans, taught by our history teacher herself to defend our independence to the death, to step over that line marked in the soil of our Republic and first and foremost, to "Remember the Alamo."

HALL OF PRESIDENTS

By my sixth-grade year, it seemed that our history teacher's purpose in life was to get us to memorize all 42 United States presidents. Mrs. Hensley taught us a song with helpful little tricks to remember all those names.

It started off with a nice marching beat to the first three presidents: George Washington, John Adams, Thomas Jefferson. When the song reached Rutherford B. Hayes, we got to practice one of the tricks. We were to linger there for a few seconds, half of us saying, "Rootherford," the other half saying, "Rutherford," back and forth, as if we were disagreeing about the pronunciation of his name. Calvin Coolidge was also in on the game. We paused on his name, saying, "Calvin, Cal, Coolidge, Cool," making a wavy "cool" hand motion during the latter part.

All of this prep work would culminate in an event, the

Hall of Presidents, held in front of an audience of parents and friends on Presidents' Day in February. My classmates and I each had to select a U.S. president or a spouse, dress up as that pubic figure and perform a speech before our audience.

Julia Poppy, so enamored with the hand motion in the song, chose to represent Calvin Coolidge, while Kevin Whitley, the tallest boy in our class and the only one with enough peach fuzz on his chin, picked Abe Lincoln, top hat and all.

As for me, I chose Barbara Bush, wife of former President George H.W. Bush. Mom helped me decide, noting that since my grandmother had given me three strands of pearls, Mrs. Bush would be an excellent woman to portray. As an added incentive, Mrs. Bush, during her term as First Lady, had flown onto the Hidden Plains campus to promote her childhood-literacy campaign.

I was awestruck upon seeing her private helicopter touch down in the school parking lot, where we stood to greet her at a safe-enough distance from the helicopter. I asked her to autograph my copy of *Millie's Book: As Dictated to Barbara Bush*, authored by her springer spaniel, Millie. I stared at her three-strand pearls for those few seconds that passed in slow motion. That could go in my speech, Mom told me.

And so I set out on my duty and privilege of playing both First Lady and speechwriter until finally the day of the Hall of Presidents had arrived. I wore a red, knee-length, wool dress with a white-and-blue sailor collar, very Betsy Ross, and three strands of freshwater pearls draped across my outfit perfectly. I truly looked the part. To top it all off, Mom had poured an entire package of Arm & Hammer baking soda into my light-brown hair to mirror the hair of "the Silver Fox."

When it was time to step up to the microphone, I began

my speech with, "Good afternoon. My name is Barbara Bush, and I am the wife of the 41st President of the United States, George Herbert Walker Bush. I was born in Rye, New York, and I like to play tennis and do needlepoint. I am passionate about promoting literacy in America."

At that moment, I started to cough, and then choke on my words. I couldn't even see the handwritten, cursive words lining my notebook paper. Apparently, baking soda prefers to fall out of one's hair, rather than cooperating by staying put in it. My allergic eyes started to itch, and each time I gasped for breath, I swallowed my choke.

I struggled to finish my speech, but seeing the audience members grimace and wince in commiseration, I ran off the stage into the girls' bathroom. Thankfully, this was a friendly political crowd, so there were no objects hurled or obscenities uttered in my direction.

Some of my friends followed me into the restroom, my dignity trailing me in a cloud of flying, white powder with every step. They tried to console me while wiping speckles of white matter off of my shoulders. And that's when I realized that political life isn't all it's cracked up to be.

As our country's First Lady, Barbara Bush might have known what it was like to be under constant surveillance and to be criticized for her acerbic wit. But during my one-day career as Barbara Bush as our country's First Lady, only I could recount what it was like to have an audience watch you choke on what could either be some serious stage fright or a bad case of dandruff.

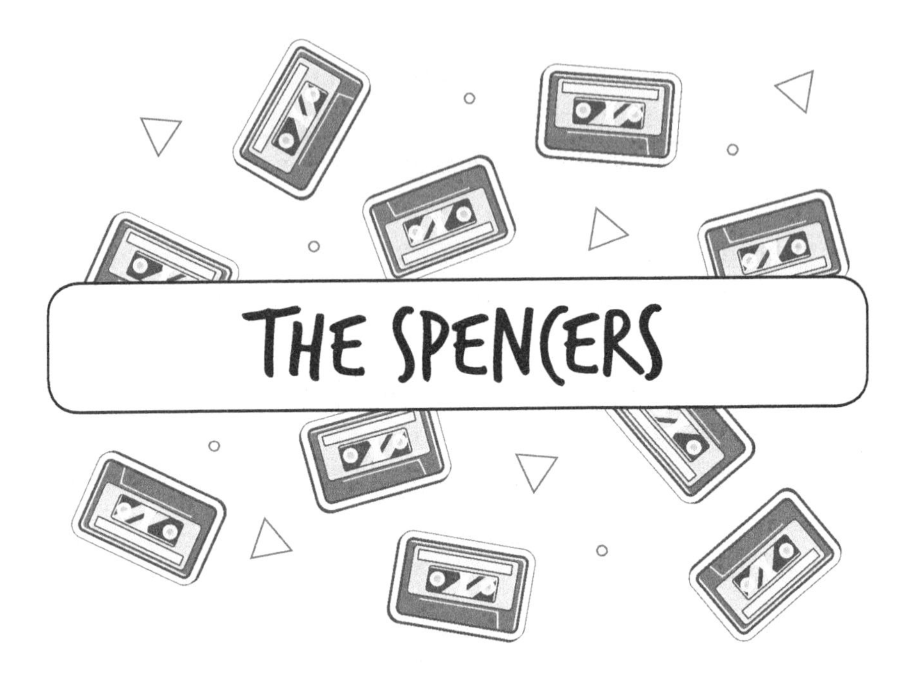

THE SPENCERS

Donna Spencer had a constant twinkle in her eye, like a mischievous teenage boy in a middle-aged-woman's body. Her daughter, Nikki, became one of my best friends at Hidden Plains, but it was Donna who made our adolescence an adventure.

When the Spencers moved to town during my sixth-grade year, I could tell based on first impressions that they were a family I'd like to know. Donna Spencer owned a chain of fitness centers in Arizona called Ripped Physique, and she coined the gym's motto, "Get ripped or get goin'." She wore sweatshirts around the house and around town featuring the gym's tagline, which she loved to repeat to anyone within earshot.

Donna was incredibly fit. Everywhere she went, she sported jean shorts cuffed to her upper thigh. She was no stranger to the tanning bed, which only augmented the definition of her toned physique.

Nikki's dad was a respected radiologist in town. He too strived for fitness perfection, and in no time a local health-food restaurant named a dish in his honor. The Lou Burger, as it was called, consisted of so many vegetables that I can only assume that he was the one patron who ordered it.

Kristen Bennett and I quickly discovered that Nikki's house was equivalent to freedom and happiness, so we asked our parents if Donna could pick us up some weekdays from school. We were surprised to learn that despite being a a heath nut, Donna would let us eat whatever we wanted, which at that time was any fried menu item McDonald's could supersize.

Each afternoon, we rushed through the drive thru so we could run upstairs to Nikki's room and watch episodes of *Saved By the Bell.* We scarfed down our fries, our eyes transfixed on dreamy Zach Morris with his 1990s cell phone that extended from above his head to below his chin.

Many times, Donna took Nikki, Kristen and me to Putt-Putt, where we played miniature golf and arcade games to our hearts' content. When she dropped us off, Donna gave us what seemed like a fortune of $60 to spend freely and $20 to spend only in case of an emergency. Time and time again, we located an "emergency," most often the giant claw in a glass container that allegedly could grip onto a stuffed animal, though it never did for us. My mom scowled whenever she passed what she called "the ripoff machine" at a movie-theater arcade.

Other times, we preferred frolicking through the giant, indoor jungle gym called Exploration Haven. It was the kind of place where kids ran wild and threw multicolor, plastic balls at each other's faces. I saw far too many portly boys get claustrophobic or altogether stuck inside the interconnecting crawl tubes that were meant to be an escape, not a destination.

Exploration Haven also housed arcade games, like the crocodiles that dodged being beaten over the head with a mallet. This was where the three of us spent most of our time because we knew that if we excelled, the machine would spit out tickets, which we could exchange for prizes.

Our proudest achievement was the time we saved up enough tickets to buy a life-size, stuffed tiger wearing a purple turban. He was supposed to look like the princess's tiger in the movie *Aladdin*, but he must have been subject to a production malfunction because he bore more of a resemblance to the film's scheming villain.

Still, we had to have him, and we promised each other we would share him, trading him off in weeklong increments to live at each of our houses. It worked for a few weeks, but Sultan must have grown accustomed to the Spencers' lifestyle because he set up permanent residence in Nikki's bedroom.

Though we were just 12, Donna found a loophole to let us start driving well before the legal age. She bought Nikki a go kart, the kind that rose only a few inches above the pavement. The entire summer we cascaded down their paved alley, wide enough to be used as a two-lane road. We attached a tiny, triangular flag of surrender to the go kart's antenna in case an oncoming vehicle failed to slow down for our sputtering contraption. We felt way ahead of the curve, scooting along at 5 miles per hour, waving at Nikki's neighbors as they pulled into the garages of their spacious estates.

Kristen's family was going through a difficult time that year, and Donna tried to make the holidays extra special for her. Kristen had nagged her mom Sue for a TV in her bedroom, but Sue kept giving her a consistent, firm decision of no.

When Donna heard about the situation, she hightailed it to Walmart and called Sue from the home-entertainment section, boldly suggesting that if Sue didn't buy Kristen a TV, she would right then and there. Sue was indignant and informed Donna that the buying would remain inside the Bennett family. Sue did let Kristen have a TV, albeit the tiniest one I had ever seen. I really had to squint to even identify which program was playing on the screen.

Full of holiday cheer that year, Donna visited a Christmas store and drove home with her very own life-size polar bear. He may have blended in among his Arctic peers, but wearing a Santa hat and standing tall at the Spencers' front door, towering over any middle-school guest that would come over for a slumber party, well, he stood out here in Texas.

Each day, he was dressed in the same outfit and maintained the same expressionless face as he greeted visitors at the door. He looked like a butler and acted like a mime. Donna beamed as she pulled us aside and confided, "Girls, I bought him with my money, not Lou's money. A woman should always have money of her own. Remember that."

News spread quickly in our class of 18, and all the girls wanted to be invited to one of Nikki's slumber parties. Unsupervised in the basement, we could watch a marathon of movies and stuff our faces with junk food.

For exercise, we ran up the basement stairs into the kitchen, which had two entire cabinets devoted to processed sugar and preservatives. Neon-pink-and-yellow Peeps ducks, artificially flavored fruit snacks and creamy marshmallow treats spilled from the shelves. I grabbed handfuls and skipped downstairs, not wanting to miss a moment of the action.

The Spencers didn't rent movies, they bought movies, even ones they hadn't seen yet. The entire back wall of their basement consisted of films of all genres. Forget Blockbuster, the Spencers were our video store.

A copious number of cats lived with the Spencers, some of them strays that they had adopted. Freddy, a male cat who sported a pink cast after a fall on the stairs, liked to situate himself on my face in the middle of the night. I woke up the next morning to a swollen-shut right eye, and it was then that I learned of my severe cat allergy.

Forced to choose between the Spencers' 12 live-in cats or my full range of vision, I chose the Spencers. From then on, Donna sequestered a box of Sutafed strictly for me in the mornings.

She must have wanted to compensate for the inconvenience because, unbeknownst to us, Donna enrolled Nikki, Kristen and me in the boxer-of-the-month club. This was back in the day when preteen girls wore boxers as shorts out on the town, though we did have to wear underwear also because of the openings for males.

I was never so happy to check the mailbox. Once a month, I received a pair of boxers, each one with a different theme. There were smiley-face boxers in September, shamrocks in March and lobsters in June.

But when it came to outdoing herself, Donna had barely hit her stride. It was time to prepare for the annual Hidden Plains lip-sync contest. And when Donna got that look in her eyes, like a cheetah catching sight of an unsuspecting gazelle, I knew the grand prize would be ours.

ELVIS "THE PELVIS" PRESLEY

"Hello, parents, students and guests. Welcome to the annual Hidden Plains Halloween carnival," Fiona Decker, our sixth-grade volleyball coach, said into the microphone.

"As y'all know, we open the carnival with a lip-sync contest," she continued. "The rules are simple. Each individual or group of performers must be in costume and have one song prerecorded on a cassette tape. Performers can dance to the music, but no singing allowed." She scanned the room, squinting, as she said to the parents, "Don't think for a minute that I won't disqualify your sweet, little darlings for breaking the rules." Then, she blew her whistle for five seconds. "Good luck," she said.

Nikki Spencer, Kristen Bennett and I were up. Sweat began to soak the armpits of my skin-tight, white, polyester jumpsuit with huge, gold stars lining the exterior. We had practiced for weeks, ever since Nikki's mom Donna finished constructing our costumes by hand.

Coach Decker inserted the cassette tape. A few moments of static filled my eardrums, but finally I heard the music.

"I think I'm gonna throw up," I said.

"Just remember when Donna taught us to swivel our hips like the King," Kristen said.

Elvis's deep voice boomed throughout the gym. Parents howled. Judges' jaws dropped. All eyes were on us, three 12-year-old girls in white, polyester jumpsuits and jet-black Elvis wigs with extra-long sideburns.

The heat of the artificial, neon stage lights sent streams of sweat racing down my jumpsuit like they were swimming for Olympic gold. Polyester doesn't breathe, and I feared that the rows of tiny, flashing Christmas-tree lights Donna had sewn into our costumes would combust from my perspiration. I closed my eyes and envisioned myself in Nikki's cozy living room, where Donna had taught us to dance like Elvis "the Pelvis" Presley.

"Now, girls, you'll be lip synching to 'Heartbreak Hotel,' which was recorded in 1956," Donna said. "TV viewers couldn't see below Elvis's waist because his pelvis thrust was offensive to mainstream America."

"Does that mean we're not supposed to thrust?" I asked.

"Oh, no, just the opposite," Donna said. "You must thrust with gusto and swivel your right hip like this." She demonstrated with hyperbolic, circular hip motions.

"Uh, Donna, you're swiveling a lot more than just your right hip," Kristen said. "You're shaking your booty and your knee and your left hip too."

"It's the art of exaggeration," Donna said. "Now, America

couldn't see him swivel those hips on TV, so what did Elvis do, Nikki?"

"The lip curl," Nikki said. "Like this."

Nikki lifted only the right side of her upper lip so high it was almost even with her nose. Donna's eyes expanded. "Exactly," she said. "And here's the clincher, how we're going to win the contest. What does every king need? A queen. Elvis always focused on someone in the audience, singing to her alone. Nikki, near the end of the song, you're going to sway toward Coach Anthony. Croon to him. I mean really get in his face."

The thought relaxed me, and I opened my eyes. Right on cue, Nikki sashayed toward the judges' table, where Coach Anthony, the boys' basketball coach who made his players run laps until their light-red shirts turned crimson, sat stone-faced in a metal folding chair.

The minute Nikki the Pelvis worked the upper lip curl and mouthed the lyrics to Coach Anthony, his stare softened. His shoulders bobbed up and down he was laughing so hard.

"Donna is a genius, it's in the bag," Kristen whispered, her pelvis gyrating to the beat.

"Yeah, no sweat," I said in a muffled tone so that Coach Decker couldn't hear me.

HOW I BECAME A VEGETARIAN

There was some bad blood between the Spencers and meat. The entire family was 100% vegetarian, including their 12 cats. Lou Spencer was a radiologist, so they all were vigilant about their inner health.

Donna Spencer was a health nut and a friend to all animals. She often belted out the song "Colors of the Wind" from *Pocahontas* when Kristen and I visited their house. Donna's favorite lyrics mentioned that the moon was blue and something about a smiling bobcat.

Donna told us, with much feeling, "This song understands me," and she tried to help us girls strengthen our appreciation of nature.

With 12 cats roaming around the Spencers' house, I definitely felt one with nature. Estella Spencer, Nikki's older sister, was a gymnast who ventured off to train in Ohio. Her reason for not eating meat tied in with her rigorous training. As a carbon copy of Donna, Nikki became a vegetarian to please her mom, though I thought she secretly envied Kristen and me for being able to indulge.

Ever since I knew the Spencers, they had vetoed meat from their dinner table in favor of salads, tofu and egg beaters, long before those foods went mainstream. Once, I went with them to IHOP, and Donna ordered two plates of egg whites with no bacon, no grease and no yolk.

The waiter looked shocked. "No bacon?" he asked.

"No," Donna said dramatically. "I don't eat household pets."

He stared at her blankly. "Ma'am, what *do* you want on your order?" he asked in all seriousness.

The Spencers occasionally tried to convert others to vegetarianism. First, Nikki told me I shouldn't drink chocolate milk. I found this curious, since they stocked their refrigerator with regular, white milk. They obviously weren't against milk in its natural state. I told Nikki that I liked chocolate milk and would continue to drink it.

Then, one time when Kristen and I spent the night at the Spencers' house, Nikki came up with the farfetched notion that chocolate milk was cow's blood.

That did it. Every time I took a sip, I imagined drinking blood straight from a cow's udder. My weak stomach won out, and I stopped drinking chocolate milk.

Another time after school, Kristen, Nikki and I went to McDonald's, where Kristen and I ordered chicken nuggets.

"You shouldn't eat chicken, you know," Nikki said.

"Why not?" I asked.

"Chicken breast is from a living, breathing being," Nikki said. "That chicken is a mother. How would you feel if someone ate your mother's chest from a paper sack and dipped your mother's chest in artificial ketchup?"

"I never thought about it that way," I said.

"Well, you should," Nikki said. "You're splitting up a family."

After that, remorseful thoughts plagued my mind every time I ate chicken. I imagined the families, a baby chicken's waving goodbye to its mom. So I switched to Texas beef, and the next time we ordered McDonald's, I got a hamburger on the kids' meal.

Apparently, Nikki had less affection for cow families than chicken families. I was stunned when she said, "Let me try a bite of your hamburger."

"What?" I asked her.

"I've never tasted red meat, and it smells good. I just want to try a tiny bite," she said. "Please?" This from the mouth that once told me I was drinking cow's blood?

We were sitting at the Spencers' dining-room table, imported from Italy with elegant place settings for 12. The three of us felt like royalty eating our McDonald's on Donna's china as we watched game shows on TV.

I passed Nikki my hamburger, and she took a small bite, circulating it through her mouth like a cow's chomping on a blade of grass. I wondered if she would spit it out, but she swallowed the whole bite.

Nikki hesitated for a few seconds.

"What do you think?" I asked.

She didn't say a word, but she did answer my question. Huge chunks of vomit erupted from her mouth, spreading across more than half of the dining-room table. A days' worth of food dripped off the polished wood surface, landing on the floor and my open-toed shoes.

Never again did I see Nikki eat a morsel of meat, but then again, I didn't either. My squeamish stomach emerged victorious once again, and that's the story of how I became a vegetarian.

CAFETERIA

All throughout my school days, I remember spending large amounts of time in the school cafeteria, not just because we ate lunch there but also because we had chapel services and basketball games there too.

During chapel, Hidden Plains students flipped through our hymnals and studied for tests while we were supposed to be paying attention to the chaplain. The acolytes were busy trying not to light anyone's hair on fire with their candles, and after chapel, Mario and Luis had to remove the breakfast some kid vomited during the benediction.

The stench of puke was still in the air during afternoon basketball practices. The aroma of sweaty bodies, uniforms that needed washing and more vomit, the aftermath of running sprints, joined the already unpleasant quality of our air. It was only fitting that middle-school students would have to eat lunch in there.

The remnants of its previous uses were evident. The rolling carts of hymnals and psalm books sat in the corner by the janitor's closet, and the scoreboard and basketball goals never were lowered. Mario and Luis rolled back the rows of bleachers to make way for the long tables where we ate lunch every weekday at 12:15 p.m. sharp.

By that time, the cafeteria housed the distinctive combination smell of burning wax from the chapel candles, sweat from our uniforms that begged for a good soak in the washing machine and whatever was frying in grease ready to be served up in the lunch line.

At least our lunch ladies' faces were pleasant and familiar. Several Hidden Plains moms and one dad, *my* dad, took turns working the lunch line, which doubled as our concession stand during basketball games. A row of moms, ranging in height from 5'2" to 5'8", and one 6'3" man, all of them in hairnets, slopped spoons full of cole slaw and the dreaded Sloppy Joe sandwich, a conglomerate of various beef parts put to a grinder, onto the neatly divided sections of our white, Styrofoam lunch trays.

"Hi, Dad," I mumbled as I passed through the line.

During the preteen years, the last thing a girl wanted to be was different, and having your dad wear an apron and fork over mashed potatoes at school definitely was considered different. Because of my untamed, wild-horse type of reaction, Dad couldn't afford to repeat what he had announced once to Mom and me, that he wanted to trade his job at the furniture store for Mom's volunteer job of serving in the cafeteria line and picking up Kristen and me from school. Dad changed his mind when his own dad was even more freaked out by the idea than Mom and me.

Hidden Plains students had to eat lunch in 30 minutes or less, which is how I developed a lifelong habit of engulfing a banana in two bites and swigging my container of milk in one gulp. It seemed almost criminal to make kids eat that fast, except that we were grouped by a preassigned seating chart with members of our grade levels to add a social component to lunchtime.

Kristen Bennett, Jasmine Pine, Becca Stafford, Julia Poppy and Nikki Spencer were my best friends, but sadly for me, they all were assigned to the other end of the table. They sat together on one end of the long cafeteria table, while I was sequestered at the other end of the table with Logan Walsh, Paul Townsend, Josh Sheridan and Andy Scott, all boys and all delinquents by the Hidden Plains standard of decorum.

I tried to sit quietly and eat my healthy fruit and sandwich that Mom had tucked neatly into small, plastic Ziploc bags. All I wanted to think about was the memory of the previous night, when Mom and I had used different cookie-cutter shapes to create miniature, peanut-butter-and-jelly sandwiches shaped like the state of Texas and Christmas bells, but the rowdy boys seemed to delight in invading my space.

With one hand strategically placed behind his neck, Logan screamed, "Hey, Ashley, I'm bleeding," and suddenly, blobs of blood squirted onto my face and shirt. Unbeknownst to me, Logan had opened five packets of ketchup with his teeth, spitting the "open here" labels behind him. He clasped the packets behind his neck and squeezed them with one firm grip, sending streams of "clotted blood" onto my face and my food, which had looked so appetizing a few moments before.

The boys all clapped and agreed it was hilarious, except for Josh, who was too busy licking his golf-ball-sized jawbreaker, which was mostly white with flecks of green, blue and red that stuck out along the shell.

Elvira Burns, our unofficial lunch police, marched over and told Paul, Logan and Andy that they had been assigned clean-up duty. They all stood up at the same time, and the loss of their weight caused the table to fold up in the middle, which sent my female friends sliding down one side of the table and Josh Sheridan and me sliding down the other end to the cafeteria floor.

Resuming our seats at the lonely end of the table, Josh and I sat across from each other in silence. I wiped away my fake blood, and Josh continued to lick his way to the jawbreaker's core. He must have felt a wave of compassion for me because he looked into my eyes and extended his right hand, offering me the chance to help him get to the center of his candy, which hadn't appeared to diminish in size.

"No thanks," I said, trying to gauge my gag reflex.

"How many licks do you think it will take to finish off this jawbreaker?" he asked.

"Thousands probably," I said.

"Maybe, but mark my words, I'm going to finish it before the end of lunch," he said. "Hey, want to see something cool? I don't have a thumbnail. I busted it on my skateboard."

Sure enough, where most people had a thumbnail, Josh Sheridan had only the quick of his nail bed, which was solid black and blue from the impact of his skateboard crash. For a few seconds, my gaze shifted back and forth between Josh's multicolored, overworked tongue, still in constant motion, and his black-and-blue thumb, yearning for the protection and sturdiness of a thumbnail. Then, I had to excuse myself to go curb my nausea in the girls' restroom.

The only redeeming factor of that day was walking back to class and seeing Logan, Paul and Andy take turns spraying bleach and wiping the cafeteria tables and floors with dish towels. All three of them were sticky with remnants of Sloppy Joe-sandwich day in the Hidden Plains lunchroom. Elvira Burns hovered over their backs and said every so often, "You missed a spot."

From that day forward, I stopped complaining about the hastiness of our lunch break. Thirty minutes alongside Logan, Paul, Josh and Andy suddenly seemed like plenty of time in the Hidden Plains cafeteria.

Food

I always loved to eat, but growing up, I was not a morning person, and you could say I took out my crankiness on breakfast foods. Despite Mom's best efforts to prepare me for school with a hearty breakfast, I preferred to scarf down a few bites of cereal on my way out the door.

That said, the smell of butter and cinnamon or anything that awakened my senses could win over my affection. I was a sucker for Mom's cinnamon toast, which was what alerted me to get up for real from the early morning nap I took after my alarm clock had sounded 30 minutes before.

Mom sent me out the door with a $1 bill, which was my snack money for the vending machines, and the neon-orange, packaged fries I bought for $.65 were the highlight of my whole day. By midmorning at school, I was regretting the decision to skip breakfast.

Officially, snack time started at 10:30 a.m., but my stomach, it seemed, couldn't wait that long. It started to tell me so during chapel around 8:30 a.m., when it began growling very loudly.

I tried to make my mind reason with my stomach. "Stop it," I said. "You're embarrassing me."

My classmates actually turned around during the prayer to determine the source of the commotion and asked, "Is that your stomach?" But my stomach always had to have the loudest word, and it responded with a loud roar.

Everything was under control as long as I was walking around or not in a setting where complete silence was required. But the minute the room got quiet, my hunger pangs got loud and obnoxious.

By the time history class began, my stomach was at it again. While Mrs. Hensley lectured us about world leaders, my insides were chiding me for not feeding them sufficiently. It started with a low grumble, which sounded like a stomach belch. I lurched, hoping no one heard. Then, it grew to three growls, like a rock skipping over a pond. The sound traveled down my left side, where it echoed for everyone to hear.

I learned to position myself to shield the noise. I wrote notes with my right hand, and with my left fingers, I gripped the area of the sound, as if it were a leaky opening that needed to be plugged. I tried to trick my body into thinking that the hand that clenched the outside of my stomach was actually food that was filling the internal hollowness. The mental taxation and all of that multitasking were very constricting. I took notes, tried to focus on the lesson rather than on my stomach and struggled to appear like I wasn't stressed about the loud noises I was making.

Finally, 10:30 a.m. arrived, and it was snack time. I had two favorite options from the vending machine. One was Gardetto's trail mix, which Kristen Bennett and I divided because we each liked half of the contents. I gave Kristen the pretzels and nuts, and I kept the mini breadsticks and dark-brown pieces of dried rye bread for myself. Every day, Kristen marveled at the fact that I didn't like pretzels and nuts. Day after day, the shock of that surprise never wore off.

My other option was a package of crunchy, orange fries, a composite of mysterious ingredients, mostly air and neon-orange chemicals that disintegrated in my mouth and left a spicy-tasting film on my tongue that sustained me until lunch 90 minutes later. Jasmine Pine brought another most interesting snack option, an entire bag full of grated cheese, the sight of which almost made me lose my appetite.

For lunch in the cafeteria, my classmates and I ate Sloppy Joe sandwiches, but when Kristen and I complained enough to Mom, she started bringing us Burger King, which we ate together in Mom's car while she asked us about our mornings.

It was my favorite time of the school day to sit in the parking lot for 30 minutes, Mom in the driver's seat, Kristen in the back seat and me in the passenger seat. Mom let us order whatever we wanted, which for me was a veggie burger with only bread, a thin, yellow slice of American cheese, plus lettuce, tomatoes and ketchup. The Burger King employees were confounded that I would order a burger with no meat. They even introduced a veggie patty, but Mom said in the drive-thru lane, "She doesn't want any patty. Just bread, cheese, lettuce, tomatoes and extra ketchup." Once, we counted, and the clerk gave us 32 packets of ketchup for one order. Now that's extra ketchup.

I had a habit of eating my French fries a certain way. I laid out a napkin on the car's console and opened six packets of ketchup, which I doused with packets of pepper. I dipped my fries in the peppery ketchup, leading Kristen to ask, "You want some fries with all that ketchup?"

I washed it all down with a large Dr. Pepper and sometimes a vanilla malt for dessert. At that time, I was still "toothpick legs" and could afford the calories. No joke, I thought I was being healthy eating that for lunch because, after all, I had eliminated beef, which I perceived as the true culprit of health woes.

Mom wasn't fooled, though. On days when I ate in the cafeteria, she packed my lunch, which included a turkey sandwich and a bag of carrots. She didn't find out until years later that I traded Elise Rousseau my carrots for her decadent moon pies, which oozed chocolate and refined sugar.

Why Elise wanted my carrots I'll never know. I guess in our kitchen we were starved for junk food, whereas in her kitchen they were starved for fresh vegetables.

Either way, even though I'm now on an enlightened and healthy lifestyle of steamed fish, green veggies and fresh fruit, I'll always have special place in my heart for packets of ketchup dolloped with pepper, counterfeit-yellow, individual slices of American cheese and especially chocolate-filled moon pies trimmed with white icing.

63RD STREET DEPOT

Growing up, everyone has a favorite restaurant. Some serve pizza, others barbecue, but my favorite restaurant served some good, old-fashioned gambling for children. Oddly enough, my parents and Kristen Bennett's parents agreed to take us to 63rd Street Depot for lunch right after church most Sundays. Every other kid wanted to eat there too, and never was there an empty spot in the lot of the bustling shopping center.

"Will you let us out at the door so we can put our name on the waiting list?" Kristen and I begged.

Because we went to a Baptist church, we had the sharp disadvantage of getting dismissed 10 minutes after the other denominations. So, at 12:30 p.m., Kristen and I ran inside, and before the hostess could ask, one of us bellowed, "Vaughn, party of seven, a nonsmoking table, as soon as possible, please."

63rd Street Depot was a bar and grill with an arcade-style

game room sectioned off in the back. The seats of its red, plastic booths morphed to the shapes of our bodies. Within five minutes of climbing into the booths, Kristen and I ordered off the menu, not that we needed one.

We always ordered chicken fingers with French fries and Dr. Peppers that came in large, red cups that week after week we were tempted to walk out the door with for our enjoyment at home. Kristen and I requested so many refills that my dad would elevate his head and peer into our cups, as if to suggest they were bottomless wells of soft drinks.

Kristen and I weren't fazed. We ran off to the game room, leaving our parents sitting in the booth, all four of them childless for the next two hours. But not before completing our routine. We both sashayed over to our dads and gave them a huge grin, which was like saying, "Open Sesame" to their wallets.

Dave and Dad handed us each a $5 bill, and off we went, bumping into the tray-balancing waiters and waitresses on our way to the arcade. I marched my $5 to the token machine, straightening the bill as I headed there. There was no time to waste, since the machine immediately rejected crumpled bills.

Inserting $5 into the machine translated into a rapid stream of flowing tokens, most of which landed in a solid-metal basket. Our fingers launched toward the excess tokens before they spilled onto the floor.

And with fists full of our juvenile equivalent of poker chips, the games had begun.

To the right were the pool tables, off limits to Kristen and me because of the sketchy characters hanging around, even at lunchtime. I could practically see Mom's figure hovering over me, shaking her finger no if I got too close to the area.

Also off limits was the "ripoff machine," a glass-enclosed game featuring a giant claw that opened and closed as if it were a breathing sea creature. Raised and lowered by a crane, the claw's metal tentacles reached into the sea of stuffed animals below, their plastic eyes peering forth, pleading to be rescued.

Of course, just like a casino, "the house" usually won, which left weeping children empty-handed. Since Mom had sanctioned us from playing the game, it became all the more alluring. I think she was just afraid that I'd come home with an unlovely, stuffed hammerhead that we'd have to nurture for the next 10 years.

Kristen and I settled on Skee-Ball, the game where you roll a small, yet surprisingly heavy ball up a ramp to what looks like a bullseye, each ring painted with different point levels, 10, 20, 30 and so on. Eager to outdo each other, we inevitably sent a ball flying down the ramp, causing it to go into orbit and land clear across the room.

Then there was the crocodile game with its five empty slots randomly popping out crocodile heads that kids gleefully could hit with their mallets. Call it a child's version of an adult's need to unload the day's stress on a punching bag.

Our favorite game by far was the one where we put a token into the slot, and a motorized machine pushed it onto the lower level. If the second level, which also rotated, flicked tokens into the empty space below, the machine would spit out tickets. It was our favorite because without fail, a part would get jammed. We had to go track down an attendant, who pushed what seemed like a magic button to give us five extra tickets to keep just for the hassle of the delay.

Of course we didn't play these games just for the sake of fun or passing time. We had an end goal in sight, which was the best part of the Depot. The game room's prize counter commanded an imposing presence. Here we could take our tickets and exchange them for prizes equivalent to our success.

There were bracelets, whoopee cushions and giant stuffed animals that dangled from the ceiling. The most lucrative prizes were 24-inch television sets and an old-school telephone that was every junior-high girl's dream. It boasted a curly-q phone cord and oversized buttons with digits that lit up in florescent colors when we pushed them.

The attendant, who towered over us behind the glass cases, tapped his fingers on the counter while we stood in awe over the junky prizes. He had charge over the ticket-counting machine, which suctioned anything within six inches of the opening and displayed red numbers that darted onto its register with each ticket it collected.

For every 100 paper tickets, the attendant handed us a silver coin imprinted with a simple "100." We jumped up and down, shaking the ground, when Dad came over to tell us our food had arrived.

"Yeah, yeah, thanks Dad," I said, shooing him off so we could concentrate on more important matters than nourishing our growing bodies. He stuck out five fingers to warn us that if we didn't return to the table within five minutes, Mom would get us, and we knew she meant business. Our hearts beating fast, we feared making an impulse buy based on emotions. So we scurried to our table to scarf down our chicken fingers and fries.

I stored my tickets in a plastic Caboodles case, which boasted shocking shades of pink and purple and a turquoise handle. Every time I opened my makeshift safe, I had to dislodge a plastic button that folded in two, since the Caboodles interior split into trays and compartments. I reserved the top tray for tickets and tokens and saved the lower section for my more worthy and valuable silver coins, just like I had seen Dad demonstrate with the cash register at his furniture store. When customers handed him $50 and $100 bills, he lifted the top tray and inserted the big bills into the less exposed space underneath the drawer.

Kristen and I counted our earnings every so often. We had a habit of unloading the coins from our Caboodles onto the carpeted floor upstairs and organizing them into piles of 100s, which to our delight turned into 1000s. We recorded our grand totals on a sticky note, which I secured onto the top tray as a motivational tool for a 24-inch TV or a light-up telephone. I proceeded with my plan confidently, certain I could convince my parents to order a children's phone line once they learned I had won a free phone little by little with Dad's hard-earned money, which he forked over $5 at a time.

Years later, I learned of my parents' actual perspectives on the game room at 63rd Street Depot. Dad considered the lesson that hard work pays off, since we had to save our tickets to win a prize. Mom thought of it more like childhood gambling, wasting money that wasn't ours, collecting junk, a bad life lesson and so on.

After all, a 63rd Street Depot telephone was priced at 10,000 tickets, which probably equated to $500 or more. I guess they both had valid points, and I never did get that $500 phone.

Since Dad owned a furniture store, he took me to the telephone section and explained the value of the dollar, since Vaughn's Furniture phones were priced at $24.99. I thought of all of the other things I could buy with that extra $475.01 I'd be wasting on arcade games.

And once I decided for myself that 63rd Street Depot was a royal ripoff to scores of adolescents and an insult to my intelligence, my shockingly pink-and-purple Caboodles case wound up, just like that, in the local landfill, case closed.

MZZZ T

My classmates and I were convinced that we wanted to stay in fifth grade forever because if we moved on to sixth grade, Mrs. Henrietta Tuggle would be our science teacher. Mrs. Tuggle seemed to have hundreds of eyes all over her head, which she used to watch every move of her past, present and future students.

Everything about her was cropped and curt—her haircut, her bangs, her height and her monosyllabic words. Rumor had it she joined the church choir so that she could keep close watch on her students, looking down on us from above, her eyes focusing on ours as she mouthed the words to "How Great Thou Art." She never referred to her hymnal. In our minds, she had memorized all of the words to all the hymns as a warning that she had great mental capacity and also kept record of our good-or-bad behavior.

We sat stiff-backed in the wooden pews, not moving for an hour solid, never once having to use the restroom. Our parents mused about why they never had to reprimand us during big church when the kids who attended other schools were so squirmy.

She refused to be called anything but Mzzz T, and she shared this information on the first day of class. "Hello, my name is Mrs. Tuggle, but you can forget I ever told you that," she said. "Until you graduate, I will hereby be referred to as Mzzz T." We all took notes. The way she said it clarified that there were at least three Zs attached to the end of her title, Ms.

Mzzz T and I already were off to a rocky start. She and my sister Robin had an incident a few years prior when she asked Robin to return a stack of graded lab assignments to her classmates.

"Robby, will you pass out these papers?" Mzzz T asked. Robby was a nickname some of Robin's friends had given her.

"Sure, Henri," Robin said in response.

I haven't mentioned yet the defining characteristic of Mzzz T's appearance. In the center of her upper neck, she had a white strip that measured approximately three-inches long and one-and-a-half inches wide against the pinkness of the rest of her face and neck.

Because she often was agitated about something, Mzzz T's face-and-neck area was prone to rosiness. In this case, that something was Robin's breaking the cardinal rule of student-teacher interaction by calling her "Henri."

"Robin, go out into the hall," Mzzz T said.

Her voice was calm, but her coloring prevented any chance of hiding her wrath. A school administrator called Mom, who jumped in her car and marched into the middle-school corridor.

She agreed that Robin had erred but reminded Mzzz T that she had instigated the retort of a nickname for a nickname by addressing her as "Robby." Mom had never liked that nickname for her daughter in the first place. Robin was mortified at the time but years later appreciated Mom's rushing to her defense and pleading her case like a high-powered attorney.

So there I was years later, newly a sixth grader with that stain on my sister's, and thus my own, record. Every time I saw Mzzz T's oversized, neon Suburban, with its license plate that read "MZZZ T," pull into the Hidden Plains parking lot, I panicked.

Her aura dominated the entire middle-school hallway. She taught biology, so shipments of cases of frogs and even baby sharks appeared outside her door. The smell of formaldehyde seeped from her room into every nearby wing of the school, even into the gymnasium, where both basketball practice and lunch were held.

Many times, my teammates and I excused ourselves from the lunch line or layups to run to the bathroom and puke. And we had thought that the stench of Sloppy Joe sandwiches and our sweaty uniforms were the only things gag-worthy about the cafeteria.

When the time came for my class to dissect animals that I knew as Kermit and Tadpole, I devised a strategy. Mzzz T divided us into groups of four or five, and I arrived to my section armed with a mountain of pen and paper.

Would I like to write the report instead of cutting apart one of my former pets?

Oh, if you insist.

My ploy worked for a while. What 12-year-old boy would deny himself the opportunity to wield a scalpel in favor of the role of secretary? Eventually, Mzzz T wised up to my method and changed the rules so that everyone had to switch roles and put his or her black lab kits to use. For years, I couldn't cut a sheet of paper without thinking of those small dissecting scissors I used for tearing and peeling a frog's skin.

Finally, we moved on to the muscular system in biology. Lying on the ground over white butcher paper, we took turns drawing outlines of each other's bodies. We carefully skipped over the off-limits body parts if our partner were of the opposite sex, leaving a wavy loop in that area. As a result, our figures had extra-long torsos.

We had to identify every muscle in the body for our anatomy test. For weeks, Kristen's and my conversations revolved around triceps, biceps and the trapezius muscle. Nothing was off limits.

Test day was upon us, and we entered the classroom with total concentration. Mzzz T handed us our test packets, and the room filled with total silence. Minutes later, we heard rustling.

It sounded like clear plastic being crinkled, but there was a strict rule about no food in the biology room. The last thing we needed was a rodent infestation. After all, there were already dead frogs and sharks in there.

I peered up at Mzzz T, and her body was as stiff as ever. Her body faced straight ahead, but the marble-topped desk shielded her lower body. I tried to concentrate on my test, but the crinkling continued.

Apparently, it was distracting everyone because every few seconds a head would pop up and look around in fear that someone would be caught eating candy. We surely would have a sighting of Mzzz T's white stripe against her pink face if that were to happen.

Now, I didn't see it, but Paul Townsend swears he did. To this day, he says he stared at the wall, thinking of whether the muscle at the knee was the meniscus or the ACL, when, like a coy rabbit, Mzzz T stuffed a Twinkie in her mouth. Again and again, she robotically fed herself small pieces of Twinkies, convinced no one would notice.

Mzzz T's expertise may have been in science, but her biology class left a lasting impression on me in cinema, literature, automobiles and the monarchy.

Any name resembling hers sends chills down my longissimus thoracis, a spinal muscle included on that sixth-grade anatomy test. To me, they're Mzzzter Fonda, Mzzzter Wadsworth Longfellow, Mzzzter Ford and Mzzzter VIII of England.

For fear of the white stripe, I wouldn't even dream of calling them "Henry."

ALL I CAN SEE IS RED DAY

When my friends and I were kids, Valentine's Day was a thrill. It was sweet and innocent because we had absolutely no romantic interest in the boys in our class. The best part was that they weren't interested in us either. It was way too soon for that.

The excitement behind our yearly Valentine's Day parties at Hidden Plains revolved more around frosted cookies and brown paper sacks filled with lollipops attached to cute, tiny cards picked out by our classmates' moms.

My all-time favorite card came from little Eddie Frazier, who gave every girl in our class a Valentine with an illustration of a cow's dangling udder. Eddie signed his name below the print that read, "I'm udderly in love with you."

Poor guy, at 6 years old, he had a lot to learn about

impressing women. Mrs. Frazier, who selected the cards, had a lot to learn too.

By the time we all turned 12, Valentine's Day had changed into an anxiety-inducing experience, and the only thing that remained constant was that neither the boys nor the girls knew how to interact with the opposite sex without seeming flirtatious.

Hidden Plains renamed February 14 "All I Can See Is Red Day," and our moms planned our class's annual school party.

Jasmine Pine's mom Georgette drove to the outskirts of town to buy individually frosted, artisan-crafted cupcakes with tops featuring Cupid with his bow and arrow and giant hearts. The cupcakes caused our blood-sugar levels to spike, and we engulfed them seconds after the party began. The other moms decorated our classroom with red-and-pink-crepe-paper streamers, their faces aglow with anticipation of an afternoon of young, platonic love among the sixth-grade students.

Kristen Bennett, Nikki Spencer and I prepared for the day by going to Hidden Plains Mall and buying matching, long-sleeve shirts puff-painted with red, white and pink interlocking hearts.

During the three hours of our school party, the Hidden Plains administration allowed us to replace our uniforms with Civilian Day attire, also known as street clothes, as long as the colors were red, white or pink.

Every year, Dad made a last-minute, emergency visit to the grocery store to stock up on flowers for Mom, Robin and me. He arrived home to present roses to me a few minutes before I left for school. Men always seemed to have the more arduous role in making Valentine's Day special.

It didn't get any easier for the sixth-grade boys in my Hidden Plains class. They had two choices of gifts to purchase through the school for All I Can See Is Red Day. One option was to buy a girl a carnation or a balloon, dedicating it to her either out in the open or under the guise of a secret admirer.

My sister's classmate Chris Butler was the first boy in our school to have his own checking account, and he wrote countless $1 checks for carnations to woo all of the girls in Robin's class. The "to" and "from" names behind the purchased flower or balloon were printed in the Hidden Plains newsletter, creating much embarrassment for both the giver and the recipient. I often wondered about the reason behind the policy, since neither student wanted to have this kind of material published and distributed among the entire school population.

But nothing surpassed the humiliation factor more than singing valentines. The tradition went like this. If a boy, let's say Daniel Reid, bought a singing valentine for a girl, such as Kristen, then two male representatives from the class one year older would enter the room and announce, "We have a singing valentine for Kristen Bennett."

Both of the boys bent down one one knee, forming a makeshift bench for the girl to occupy while they sang old-fashioned love songs like "You Must Have Been a Beautiful Baby" and "Don't Sit Under the Apple Tree (With Anyone Else But Me)."

I remember one year in particular. "Anonymous" had purchased a singing valentine for me. Two boys entered the room during our class party, and I said under my breath, "Please not me, please not me."

Luke Griffin and Brent Dawson looked straight at me and said, "We have a singing Valentine for Ashley Vaughn." I turned into one of those horses who plants her hooves on the ground, refusing to budge. Emily Holland and Jasmine Pine had to push me the entire way and press on my shoulders to force me onto the boys' knees, where of course I refused to stay.

My rear balanced in midair the entire time Luke and Brent sang the lyrics. My legs shook both from anxiety and the lack of support beneath my trembling quad muscles. I looked around the room, trying to find a focal point that wasn't a pair of my classmates' eyes.

My cheeks burned until they matched the red-and-pink icing on the heart-shaped cookie cake that Mom had bought at Baskin-Robbins. Because of his rosacea, Luke Griffin's flustered cheeks coordinated with the red-and-pink decor. If we hadn't been insecure preteens too afraid to breathe around each other, we would have made the perfect pair.

But there we sat, or rather they sat with no girl on their knees to serenade because I hightailed it out the door. All of the moms considered the party a huge success. Every one of them brimmed with glee in response to young love in bloom, so much so that they were fanning themselves to contain all of their emotions.

MARIO AND LUIS

Mario and Luis were the friendly Hidden Plains janitors whose uniforms were as polished and preppy as the students' attire. Donned in all-khaki pantsuits and baseball hats embroidered with the Hidden Plains crest, Mario and Luis handled our campus maintenance issues in a swift, efficient manner.

They worked in tandem. Where there was Mario, there was Luis, and vice versa. We never mentioned one without mentioning the other. It was like the pool game "Marco Polo," in which one person had to close her eyes and call, "Marco," blindly searching with her arms until the others answered, "Polo."

Mario and Luis demonstrated their professional expertise all over campus, fighting wear and tear to our buildings with the gusto of Batman and Robin. Their first call of duty usually was cleaning up vomit after chapel, when some overstuffed student combusted the contents of his stomach onto the gym floor. The clean-up solution smelled worse than the vomit itself, but then again we were thankful for these two men who served in capacities that repulsed everyone else.

Throughout the day, we saw Mario and Luis with brooms, ladders, gardening supplies and tool belts, doing what needed to be done. We all admired that at the end of the day, our campus looked immaculate, but Mario, it seemed, had an extra-special admirer. Mario had two things working in his favor. He was a bachelor, and he wore a uniform. Ms. April Shaw, my Japanese teacher, zoomed in and took aim.

Julia Poppy and I met with Ms. Shaw twice a week after school for Beginning Japanese. We were the only two students who took a chance that the Japanese language would benefit us in the hidden plains of Texas. One week, we learned from our workbooks different family names in Japanese.

"Okasan" meant father, and "hahaoya" meant mother.

Though pleased with my new knowledge, my parents still asked, "Can't we just say 'daddy-san, mommy-san and sissy-san?'"

"Never repeat that in public or in front of my friends," I told them.

That year, Ms. Shaw was a bit distracted by a certain someone, so Julia and I were self-paced most of the time. "Konichiwa" was our go-to word, the only one we knew for sure.

Inevitably, every Tuesday and Thursday, Ms. Shaw concocted some sort of maintenance crisis, and she called in to the administrative office for maintenance help, and for Mario. To the rescue came Mario, smiling, tipping his embroidered baseball hat to Ms. Shaw as an act of chivalry.

"Ms. Shaw sure blinks a lot," Julia whispered to me.

"She's trying to bat her eyes," I whispered back.

"Girls, say konichiwa to Mario," Ms. Shaw said to us.

"Konichiwa, Mario," Julia and I said, watching their kinetic energy ignite an otherwise lackluster, drab classroom setting.

Within a few minutes, Mario repaired the minor problem and vanished. Again, he tipped his hat on the way out while Julia and I drew stick figures on our family trees and labeled them with the words "okasan" and "hahaoya."

Luis Carrillo, our head janitor, was the resident maintenance expert. If ever there was a true emergency, you wanted to call Luis. Once, a third-grade boy accidentally overflowed a toilet in the boys' restroom, and a flood of water gushed onto the floor.

As the surge headed out the bathroom door, the student followed the eye of the storm until he found Coach Chalmers, our 7'1" teddy bear of a basketball coach.

The student uttered a panicked plea to Coach Chalmers. "Call Luis," he said breathlessly. "Call Luis."

But Coach Chalmers misinterpreted his plea. "Yeah, Carl Lewis, the Olympic runner," Coach said. "You like Carl Lewis, man?"

"No, no," the student implored. "Call Luis. The toilet's overflowing out the bathroom door." So they called Luis, who saved the day once again.

Another time, Luis saved the day on my account. Once a year, we celebrated Hat Day at Hidden Plains, during which students could wear any kind of hat to school the entire day. To private-school students under heavy uniform regulations, this kind of freedom seemed like glasnost in the former Soviet Union.

That year, I chose a dalmatian baseball hat with floppy, spotted ears hanging off both sides and oversized, plastic eyes with movable pupils above the brim. After recess, I felt extra hyper, which, for a reserved teacher's pet, meant I had an ever-so-slight skip to my step.

As I skipped back to class, I removed my hat with every intention of giving it a six-inch toss into the air before catching it in my hand. Unfortunately, the strong Texas wind caught Spot before I could, and my hat wound up on top of one of the school buildings, as in the roof.

Questions swirled in my mind. Was this my most embarrassing moment? Would my classmates point and tease? Would the principal notify my parents? Would this affect my permanent record? The short-term answers were yes, yes, yes and probably yes.

While I considered the worst-case scenario--the length of my prison term and whether they'd let me off for good behavior--I noticed two figures approaching the building with my hat on the roof. It was Mario and Luis hauling a large ladder toward the area I had darted from as soon as I realized what I'd done.

I watched from inside the metal jungle gym as Luis scaled the ladder to a height that in the moment seemed like the summit of Mt. Fuji. Dependable Mario secured the base of the ladder, pulling its weight down with all of his might so that it wouldn't wobble when Luis descended toward the concrete. Thankfully, all eyes were on them instead of me, but by the time Luis's feet reached solid ground, a crowd of students and teachers had formed around them.

Luis downplayed the attention, scanning the crowd and spotting me in the distance, where I pretended to be fully occupied by the playground's monkey bars. As he neared me, my arms felt like noodles, and I dropped to the gravel, which offered little material under which I could hide.

Kindly, gently, Luis handed me my dalmatian hat like an astronaut presenting the first moon rock to NASA. He smiled, but he didn't say a word. As he walked away with his back to me, I managed to eke out a meek "thank you" in a voice as high-pitched as helium that I hoped my new superhero somehow had heard.

RIDING A BIKE

During childhood, most activities fall into one of two categories—rights and privileges. Life, liberty, the pursuit of happiness, those are rights. Mom's homemade mashed potatoes after a long day of school, picking out a new pair of shoes before the start of a new school year, those are privileges. Learning how to ride a bike also was a right, according to most kids in my neighborhood.

On Saturdays, dads would get out the bikes and lovingly, patiently coach their kids, watching them endure the pitfalls along life's road, until finally, with much tender, loving care, their youngsters mastered the art of cycling. Mashed potatoes and new outfits for all! Only that's not the way it happened in my family.

Maybe Dad did whip out the bikes on Saturday morning, but I wouldn't know because I was nowhere to be found. I made sure to secure a ride that would get me out the door before Dad knew I was awake.

Sure, I had my tomboy phase. During my homage to all-things Orlando, home of Walt Disney World, I paired a black-and-blue Shaquille O'Neal jersey with ill-fitting, neon-green-and-pink shorts. Thankfully, that stage had ended.

Now I was more of a girl's girl, risk averse, unwilling to put myself in situations that could result in a black eye or an open wound. I could be found at the mall, looking for accessories with Nikki Spencer and Kristen Bennett to accentuate our latest fashion finds, which at that moment in time centered around Tommy Hilfiger's patriotic collections.

I was a shy kid, and I loved earning girl-scout badges because I felt that each of them communicated my achievements for me. One said, "Hey, bet you didn't think I could sell 250 boxes of thin mints and peanut-butter patties, but I did."

Another said, "This trooper survived a wilderness weekend in a tent among the wolves and bears." I craved these patches because they spoke when I didn't, and I skipped in circles each time Mom sewed them onto my green girl-scout sash.

Monday marked the date of my girl-scout troop's first-annual, obstacle-course challenge. I had no idea what to expect, but I was eager to cross the finish line and accept another badge to add to my patch menagerie.

Candy Holland, our troop leader and my friend Emily's mom, tapped the microphone and announced, "Welcome, ladies, to the obstacle course. I know you've all spent many Saturday mornings with this day in mind."

Out came my first "uh oh."

"Well, here's your chance to show your stuff," Candy said. "I'm going to tell you the general overview of our course, but you'll also have to learn as you go. First, you'll run a little, so everyone make sure your shoelaces are tied. Then, you'll jump the hurdles, scale a small wall and jump through tires. Piece of cake, right?"

Well, nothing was impossible.

"Finally, you'll grab a bike and ride to the finish line," she said.

Screeeech. Bike to the finish? For this I was not prepared.

I walked over to where my parents stood. "Well, who needed that patch anyway?" I said. "Let's get out of here."

Dad put his arm around my shoulders and guided me back to the other troop members. "Give it a try, sweetie," he said gently. "You'll do great."

Candy fired the opening shot overhead with a Super Soaker water gun.

But there was no definitive sound, so Jasmine Pine's dad Edgar motioned us to move. "Go, go, go," he said.

My toothpick legs sprinted straight ahead, my nimble hips lifted my feet over the hurdles, my height surged me over the wall and my ballet balance glided me gracefully through the hopscotch tires.

I did great, just like Dad had said. Oh, but the bikes. From the sideline, Edgar released one into my possession, and awkwardly I dove on, hitting and denting every orange safety cone along the path. I advanced a few feet, but there was no pretending.

My handlebars swerved left and right, which caused extreme turbulence on my seat. I plummeted off the bike, and with my tumbling body, down went my dignity. My chin still on the pavement, I looked up at Edgar and all of the other dads.

I'm sure as parents what they felt was empathy, but their somber stares seemed to say to my shattered pride, "How could she not know how to ride a bike by now?"

Mom ran over with a First Aid kit that I wasn't aware she had brought. The next few minutes were hazy, but before too long she had sterilized, treated with ointment and bandaged probably 15 percent of my ailing body.

I stared out the backseat window on the ride home, misty-eyed and humiliated.

Dad broke the silence. "Honey, I know this seems like a really big deal right now, but it'll get better," he said. "I'm proud of you for doing the best you could."

And then I spoke. Big, big mistake.

"Well, it's your fault," I said. "Did you see the way everyone looked at me? All the other dads taught their kids how to ride bikes when they were 10."

Dad's eyes bugged out. I could see them in the rearview mirror. Screeech. This was my second reason to say "uh oh."

"Alright then," he said. "We're going to to something about that."

Dad gave me exactly one day to feel better. I taped extra squares of gauze to my uninjured elbows and shins, hoping he would back down, but this time he was steadfast.

"No more excuses," Dad said. "Today, you're learning how to ride a bike."

I peeked through the front drapes, watching him carry two bikes to the car. These were desperate times. I had nowhere to go, so I hunkered down in hiding beneath the guest-room bed. It was the only room downstairs with a bed skirt that might shield me. It was the same location the dog ran to and peed on when he escaped the laundry room, but, again, my times were desperate.

I heard Dad's footsteps. Then, his eyes peered under the bed. "Go away," I said.

"Let's go," Dad said.

"No way," I said.

I planned to stay put, even if it meant smelling dog urine all night.

Dad had other plans. He grabbed my socks and dragged me from my hiding place as if I were a human wheelbarrow. I mustered all of my strength to resist his sweeping the carpets with my back.

Slowly, we inched toward the garage, and a stinging sensation shot throughout my body. "Carpet burn, carpet burn," I screamed. Now I was infuriated. "I'll have you put away for this," I said.

"Ashley, if you don't learn to ride a bike, you won't learn how to drive a car, and if that happens, I'd never live it down," Dad said.

Mom and Dad drove me to the parking lot of our family's furniture store. Mom sat in the passenger seat and didn't get out when we arrived. Business hours were over, so the lot was a long stretch of uninhabited asphalt, the perfect place to ride bikes, if you had a willing participant.

"We're not going home until you can ride from one end to the other," Dad said. "If the employees show up tomorrow for work at 10 a.m. and we're still here, so be it."

His statement said, "I mean business." I knew he was serious because they stashed a gallon of water and some trail mix in the car. We really could have been there all night. Rarely did we see this side of Dad.

The first few rounds, I fell. One time, Dad caught my bike to keep me from a repeat injury. But this time I had my kneepads, my elbow pads and my helmet. And somewhere deep inside, I had hope, if only for a driver's license in the not-too-distant future.

The plains of Texas had the most picturesque sunsets with blues and pinks and purples cascading across the open sky. By the time I finally sailed across the parking lot, the handlebars forming a perfect, straight pattern, one of those sunsets served as the backdrop to my triumph.

I'll never forget Dad's expression in that moment. His smile expanded horizontally, and the corners of his mouth turned up, rounding out his cheeks. Big, toothy grins weren't his style. He struggled to contain his trembling lower lip and the tears that were trying to spring forth. I had never seen him look so proud.

When we pulled into our driveway at home, Nikki spotted our car from down the street at Kristen's house. They sped past the eight houses between us and rode into our driveway.

"Hey, we're going for a ride at the park," Nikki said. "Want to come?"

"Sure," I said.

Dad helped me lift one of the bikes from the trunk. Nikki, Kristen and I rode off together, fading into the horizon. Mom went inside, but Dad lingered in the driveway, soaking in the sounds of our laughter.

I wheeled in a circle and waved, making sure he knew I had noticed his presence. It was my way of telling him "thank you," despite my belligerence.

Once again, he revealed that smile, the one that emerged only when something pleased him. It was my favorite of all his expressions, and it happened to be one I had inherited.

Seeing it again thrilled me, like I had witnessed two spectacular sunsets the very same night. He lifted his chin in a nod of approval and waved back.

I knew it was his way of saying, "You're welcome."

MR. KNUTSON

Mr. Tom Knutson was our resident Renaissance man at Hidden Plains. He was our chaplain, our organist and our music teacher. He was a ticking bundle of nervous energy, and my classmates and I loved to watch his expressive mannerisms.

Mr. Knutson was a tall twig of a man, and his posture was that of a steel rod.

With his shoulders back and chest forward, the man never bent his knees or elbows while in a standing position. He parted his reddish hair straight down the middle of his head, apparently with such blunt force that the comb turned his scalp permanently pink. Either that, or Mr. Knutson secretly sunbathed every day after school.

His mustache, like his hair, was parted straight down the center, and he took careful attention to trim each side neatly and evenly. His pasty complexion resembled a porcelain doll's, and his whole demeanor could be summed up in three words: serious, regimented, focused.

During morning chapel, Mr. Knutson led the march of acolytes down the center aisle. Of the 400-500 voices that chimed in for the first hymn, Mr. Knutson could be heard above them all. He would sing the low part of the hymns and then suddenly switch to falsetto during a hymn like "Holy, Holy, Holy."

In perfect pitch, Mr. Knutson pronounced each syllable of every word with such emphatic punch that he usually was behind the crowd by a few beats. His aim wasn't harmony or unity with the audience but individual perfectionism. He had sung the hymns hundreds if not thousands of times, but whenever he passed down the aisle, he studied each note with precision and discipline as if for the first time.

When the audience finished singing the opening hymn, Mr. Knutson moved toward the organ, which he played for all subsequent hymns. He dressed in a long, white robe, the customary Presbyterian wardrobe, and tied a rope of three strands around his waist as a belt.

Mr. Knutson and the organ made quite a pair. Both instruments boomed outgoing sounds with intensity. Maximizing the length of his string-bean arms, Mr. Knutson sat a good three feet away from the organ and reached the keys by locking his elbows throughout the songs.

One song, "Joy to the Heart," ideally would be sung in two parts, with the female students singing the first round and the male students piping in for round two. Mr. Knutson sang both parts, turning his head to the left for the first round and whipping it to the right for the second round. He looked like a split-personality hymn singer with whiplash, but at least he was belting his heart out to the heavens.

Part of that same song required spanning the entire organ with his fingers in five quick beats. Mr. Knutson excelled at this action. His long right arm reached across his left arm for the low notes, and within three seconds his arms had crossed over each other, sweeping down the organ to hit the high notes. Mr. Knutson beamed in these moments, marveling at his own skillful musical prowess.

Much of Mr. Knutson's time at school was spent in the music room, where he taught music class and choir. During music class, he made us remove our red sweaters and pile them in a corner by his desk.

Eddie Frazier's sweater was a pale, faded red because it had been washed so many times, which stood out among the pool of newer, darker sweaters. Eddie's sweater was a hand-me-down from at least three of his five siblings, one of whom picked his runny nose throughout chapel and wiped his snot on the sweater.

Needless to say, I was not excited about casually piling my clean sweater in with Eddie's, knowing it might be contaminated by the time I had to put it on again at the end of class.

During music class, we used plastic recorders, the little flutelike instruments that pageboys carried in the days of yore as they whistled a tune or set out as foot messengers. We could either bring our own recorders from home or use the recycled, community recorders that Mr. Knutson supposedly cleaned after class in a blue, formaldehyde solution. I swore to Mom that those things were a cesspool of boy germs, and so she was kind enough to buy me my own recorder from the school bookstore.

Some of the boys' moms didn't seem to share Mom's compassion. Either that or they were trying to toughen them up. So there they were in music class, spitting into the same recorder that another fellow had spit into the day before. I cringed, partly in disgust and partly in empathy, whenever I saw it happen.

Mr. Knutson took class attendance the same way every day. He unfolded his roster and pulled out his own full-sized recorder, plugging the holes with his fingers and blowing into it to create his own melodies, always fast-paced, always high-pitched.

"Good morning Ashley Vaughn," he sang, repeating the melody on his recorder. That was my cue that he was registering my attendance. If I wanted to be counted present, I'd have to respond in the same pitch and melody as Mr. Knutson when he sang my name.

I didn't want to be counted absent, but I didn't want to sing in public either. I was one of those students in chapel who mouthed the words to the hymns but sounded mute to anyone within earshot.

"Good morning, Mr. Knutson," I responded, my voice quivering. Who did he think I was, Whitney Houston?

As he sang each name, Mr. Knutson extended a straight hand, hitting imaginary notes in the air, his hand going up on the high notes and down on the low notes. If his voice ventured to the key of B, so did his body. He stood on his tiptoes and reached his hand higher until it mirrored the correct note.

With his fingers perpendicular to his palm, he stopped his hand in a series of abrupt and regimented up-and-down motions, as if he were measuring the various heights of an infant, then a giant, a small child, then a full-grown adult. If Type-A personalities needed a poster boy in the 1990s, I had a good idea of where they could find one.

I really felt for the boys, whose voices would crack when they tried to emulate Mr. Knutson's high notes. Throughout music class, Logan Walsh committed the constant faux pas of using his regular speaking voice instead of his singing voice. You see, we weren't allowed to say anything during the hour if we didn't sing it.

Once, as Mr. Knutson listened to our rehearsal of a song we would perform during an upcoming chapel service, his face broke into a writing, wrenching contortion, like he had tasted poison or Hidden Plains cafeteria food. I thought he might be having a panic attack.

"Who is singing in their speaking voice?" Mr. Knutson sang despondently. His eyes zoomed in on Logan. "Are you the person singing in your speaking voice?" Mr. Knutson continued, employing the same depressing melody.

When Logan smirked, it became evident to us all that his behavior was premeditated. Still, Logan persisted, singing the words of the song in his warbling voice, sounding like a bullfrog exhibiting signs of puberty.

Mr. Knutson's face reddened in irritation. He pulled out his recorder, which was strapped into its case around his waist. Breathing into it with passion, Mr. Knutson demonstrated the proper melody to Logan, who remained obstinate in speaking, thus ruining the song's harmony.

Mr. Knutson and Logan went to battle, ready to duel to the death with their mouths. Logan warred with his off-key notes and his monotone parroting of the song. Mr. Knutson buried his face in his recorder, refusing to come up for breath as he dominated Logan with his consummate tone and pitch. Harmony and cacophony feuded for control of the classroom. The rest of us went silent when Logan broke into a singing yell.

Mr. Knutson's face reddened to a shade of maroon, not far from the scarlet sweaters piled in the corner. I looked at Mr. Knutson's face, his waning breath still going full-blast into the recorder, then shifted my gaze to the sweaters. Again, I looked at Mr. Knutson.

At that point, I saw deep, blue veins lining his face, and I figured one of us would have to run to the school nurse to request CPR. But suddenly, Logan relented.

Mr. Knutson had prevailed, and thankfully survived, though he remained visibly annoyed as he marched Logan to the principal's office. His knees and elbows locked tighter as he escorted Logan, encouraging him along by the edge of his sweater.

I always knew that Mr. Knutson's music class pushed all of my buttons. Fear of germs, check, shyness, check, singling me out in front of the class, check, check, check.

Except for the trump card we discovered shortly thereafter. Mr. Knutson lived in our neighborhood, and one evening Robin and Dad were driving through the area looking at the architecture and personality of various homes. As they meandered down the street, moving at a snail's pace, they scanned the houses to the left and right.

On the right was a house with the curtains drawn, leaving an open view through the living-room window. They both gasped as they saw Mr. Knutson, dressed only in his white underwear briefs, whistling a tune as he carried a dinner tray up the stairs, his knees and elbows locked in straight lines.

Still baffled by their innocent mistake, Robin and Dad reported the news to Mom and me as soon they got home. We all burst out laughing, and I can honestly say that Mr. Knutson lost his intimidating effect on me from that moment forward.

THE MUSIC VIDEO

Every other day, my sixth-grade classmates and I filed into Mr. Floyd Llewellyn's class, ready to endure our lot in life, two back-to-back hours of double history. We thought the material in our workbooks was dry and boring. We asked Mr. Llewellyn, whom we secretly called Floyd behind his back, when in our lives we would ever need to recite from memory the Preamble to the Constitution.

"Ahhhh," Mr. Llewellyn said. It seemed he started most every sentence with some variation of "ah" or "uh," and he always addressed his students by "Mr." or "Miss," even though we were 12. "You never know, Mr. Townsend, but please think of me when you do," Mr. Llewellyn said. The sound of Mr. Llewellyn's voice was like a foghorn combined with a bad impression of Donald Duck.

It became Mr. Llewellyn's custom to begin each history

class by asking Kristen Bennett the same question. "Ahh, Miss Bennett, what is the date of America's independence?" he asked. The first time, Kristen had no idea. The second time, someone helped her with the answer, giving her clues like "fireworks" and "summer barbecues."

"The 4th of July?" she asked dubiously.

"Correct," Mr. Llewellyn said. "Of which year?"

That she never could remember. "Umm, well, uhhh," she said, carefully mulling over her best guess.

As the 120 minutes droned on to Mr. Llewellyn's monotone voice, we all managed our boredom in different ways. Holly Gallagher sat at the back of the room, where she rearranged the keys on Mr. Llewellyn's fossil of a computer that collected dust in the corner despite the fact that he actually used it to type lesson plans. With Holly's help, the "a" key became an up arrow, the "s" key became a dollar sign and "enter" became "delete."

Cynthia Merritt stared out the window until Mr. Llewellyn caught her red-handed in a daydream. "Uhhh, Miss Merritt, please stop staring at the animals in the field," he said.

"Mr. Llewellyn, the blinds are closed," Cynthia said. It was true, but that didn't stop her from staring at the window.

"Ahhh, okay, that's beside the point, Miss Merritt," he said. "Uhh, never mind, just please pay attention."

As for Nikki Spencer, Kristen and me, we tried to remain mentally present and focused during school hours, but when evening came, we responded to a day of ennui as any red-blooded American girls in middle school might. We choreographed dance moves to our favorite pop songs and performed onstage in the space next to the den as Dad and

Mom recorded our creative progress with their home movie camera.

That year, the Spice Girls were at the height of their popularity. Nikki, Kristen and I were a group of three to the Spice Girls' five, but our energy level bridged the gap. If it had to be a Mr. Llewellyn kind of day, we were going to make it a Spice Girls kind of night.

First, we picked our song, "Spice Up Your Life." Then, we choreographed our moves and walked through a quick rehearsal. Finally, we were ready for the big show. We just needed an audience. "Dadddd and Mommm," I said, beckoning for our audience members.

"We're ready," they said. We named Dad as the cameraman, a very important role since we would watch our recording repeatedly after dinner for our own vanity and entertainment. Showtime. The lyrics boomed over the kitchen speakers, encouraging us to add zest to our lives. When the song was over, the three of us were pretty pleased with our performance.

"Nice moves," Mom said. "You girls are natural performers."

"Yeah, that was great," Dad said. "Maybe someday you'll have a bigger audience."

"Thanks," I said. "This sure beats Floyd's double history class."

"Yeah, could the man be more boring?" Nikki asked.

"Why does he always have to ask me the same question about...I can't even remember," Kristen said.

"Ahh, Miss Bennett, what is the date of America's independence?" Nikki and I asked, mimicking Mr. Llewellyn's voice. "And the year?"

"Floyd?" Dad asked. "You mean Mr. Llewellyn?"

"What's wrong with Mr. Llewellyn?" Mom asked. "I like Mr. Llewellyn."

We stared at them incredulously.

"Well, maybe he's a little different," Dad conceded.

But Mom acted as if we had insulted the beloved family pet. "You girls should be nice to him," she said. "His voice is a little hard to stomach, but he's a brilliant man."

"And a great teacher," Dad said. "Teachers like that are why parents send their kids to Hidden Plains."

"Ashley, I want you to make a special effort to say something nice to him tomorrow," Mom said.

"Mommm," I moaned in objection.

"As a special favor to me," Mom said. And that was final.

The next day, as Mom dropped us off at school, we saw Mr. Llewellyn on his bike, signaling a right turn by extending his right hand.

Mom waved to him and looked over at me. "Remember," she said.

Mr. Llewellyn fumbled into class in his usual manner. The wind against his bike had blown his tie over his shoulder and restyled the few segments of hair he had left, which now stuck straight up. One of the lenses from his glasses was missing.

Say something nice, say something nice, I reminded myself. "Hi, Mr. Llewellyn," I said, smiling. There. "Hi" was friendly. I was being nice.

"Uhh, hello, Miss Vaughn," he said. "I got the nicest note from your mom at the school office this morning. She volunteered to record the history program about the Revolutionary War that we'll be watching in class tomorrow."

"Oh, how...nice," I said.

The minute I jumped in the car after school, I begged Mom

to stop butting in on my school life. "That's so embarrassing," I said. "It's like you want to be a student again and do homework and take tests. Didn't you already go to sixth grade like 70 years ago?"

"Very funny," Mom said. "And it hasn't been quite that long since I was in sixth grade."

Still, Mom recorded the program on a VHS tape, which she sent with me to class the next day. Mr. Llewellyn was so pleased. He rewound the tape and inserted it into the VHS player. A few seconds of black-and-white sizzles appeared on the screen before the tape cut to the music video of Nikki, Kristen and me singing a hyped-up version of "Spice Up Your Life."

My classmates, especially the boys, erupted in laughter. Worst of all, I was in this alone. Kristen was absent that day, and Nikki was at the doctor getting her twice-a-month allergy shot. It was worse than a nightmare.

"Mr. Llewellyn, please stop the video. Please! I'm begging you, please turn it off," I said, almost in tears. Meanwhile, Mr. Llewellyn's head was bobbing up and down in sync with his shoulders as he laughed.

I could feel the pressure welling in my tear ducts and my cheeks reddening with each drop to the floor and every high kick that appeared on the TV monitor.

"Looks like Sporty Spice has a sunburn," Paul Townsend said as soon as he noticed I was blushing.

Finally, far too late, Mr. Llewellyn walked to the television and powered off the monitor. In an instant, the horror was over, but the shock remained.

The joy and glory of two nights prior, when Nikki, Kristen and I celebrated our first successful music video single had taken a nasty detour into that day's humiliation, notoriety... infamy. Our desire for singing careers had soured, and before long we returned to complaining about two-hour lectures and having to recite the Constitution's Preamble to an audience of Donald Duck with a foghorn.

But it's safe to say that for a brief time during the spring semester of our sixth-grade year, Nikki, Kristen and I had our moment in, well, history.

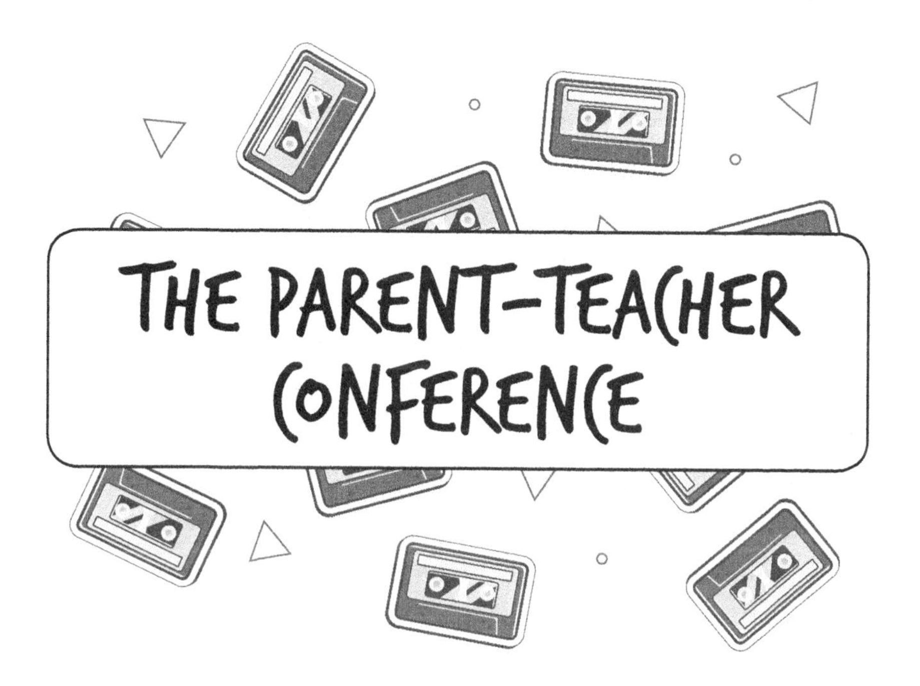

THE PARENT-TEACHER CONFERENCE

Mrs. Marjorie Sweeney, my reading teacher, had spent weeks trying to contain the noise level in her classroom, especially that of the unruly boys. Just before weekends or holiday breaks, they would act out by doing things like shooting spit wads from behind their desks into Amy Johansson's thick piles of long, brown curls.

Each morning before school, Amy woke up two hours before she had to leave her house so she could have time to wash and blow dry her hair. Then, she would start the elaborate styling process of curling her hair with a curling iron, flipping her head up and down 20 times to loosen the curls, curling them again with hair rollers and finally jumping up and down for a full minute to give it body, volume, life.

Life it had, but unfortunately it was the kind of living bacteria that came from the saliva of Brandon Prescott II's and Reagan Ingram's spit wads. Amy's hair took up almost an entire zip code, so she never knew what hit her.

"Class," Mrs. Sweeney said, tapping her ruler against her desk. "I've come up with a system to reward good behavior." She cleared her throat and glared at Brandon and Reagan. "Over on the wall, you'll see a white poster board and a list of all your names," she said. "If I have to reprimand a student, I'll write your name on the chalkboard, and you will not get a gold star on the poster board."

She went on to say that whenever we got 15 stars next to our individual name on the poster, we would celebrate one week by ordering in lunch from Greasy Goodness Cafe. Those who earned anything less than 15 stars had to report to the cafeteria for lunch. Mrs. Sweeney knew how to motivate us.

Greasy Goodness Cafe represented the eternal goodness of junk food--the fragrant smells of curly fries and genuine angus burgers and the majesty of 32-ounce Dr. Peppers that gave us the same look of strength as Lady Liberty. We might have to make five afternoon bathroom visits from stuffing that many solids and liquids into our stomachs, but it was worth it.

Suddenly, visions of the sweat-infused cafeteria disappeared. The remainder of my school year would be filled with endurance, purpose and grass-fed beef.

For the next two weeks, I tried my hardest. Not that it took much effort. I already had a pattern of starting my homework the minute I got home from school. I was never late to class, I rarely missed a day of school and my teachers loved me.

How did I know this? My parents reported back with the results of their parent-teacher conferences. Traditionally, my parents let me wait in the car. I'd be halfway into the first chapter of my book, when they would emerge, holding hands, not a care in the world.

"Well, Mrs. Sweeney said you're not perfect, but you're about as close as a sixth grader can get," Dad said. "You turn in your homework ahead of the due date, you sit in the front row of class, you never speak without raising your hand and you've already written book reports on the summer reading list," Mom beamed. "You make our job as parents look easy. What do you say we celebrate with burgers and curly fries from Greasy Goodness Cafe?"

I was pretty satisfied, grinning and wagging my tail like a well-heeled poodle trotting to accept my gold medal at the Westminster Kennel Club Dog Show. After we returned home from celebrating at Greasy Goodness Cafe, I completed my homework, due the following week.

The next day at school, I was minding my own business, daydreaming about the end of the day, when I would earn my 15th star and partake in meaty, greasy, syrupy paradise. And that's when it happened.

I looked at the chalkboard. Written in all-capital letters, practically a nod to the flashing lights and bright glare of a police siren, was my name...ASHLEY.

Kristen Bennett gasped. Jaws dropped. Clocks froze. Most amazingly, Brandon Prescott II, for the first time all year, stood in complete silence. He must have been shell-shocked. Everyone wondered the same thing. What could Ashley possibly have done wrong?

I tried to hold back my tears all afternoon, but as soon as I was home, the waterworks erupted like a geyser. I processed the day's events aloud with Mom and Dad. "I was just sitting there...just like always...and my name...and the board...in ALL CAPS...so humiliating," I said.

And then, I looked up from the floor and asked the question that mattered most. "Do you think this will go on my permanent record?"

I could imagine the college admissions board's reviewal of my application.

"Yearbook staff, fluent in French, basketball captain. Princeton would be glad to welcome such a fine student," one of them would say. "Except, what's this?"

"Well, that looks like a spot on her permanent record," another board member would say, eyeing the sheet of paper with a magnifying glass. "In sixth grade, she got her name on the board...in ALL CAPS."

"And underlined," they would say, pausing to gasp before stamping the word "DENIED" on my application.

"Oh, honey, no," Mom said. "That permanent record nonsense is what they tell boys like Brandon to scare them into behaving. I'll make you some mashed potatoes, and we'll talk to Mrs. Sweeney tomorrow. We'll sort this out."

I loved this lady. And truly, her homemade mashed potatoes did make me feel better because she fixed them just the way I liked, with milk and butter served in a bowl where you could still taste small chunks of potato.

Mom was so relaxed and comforting. Dad, on the other hand, paced nervously and was silent. "Can I talk to you in the other room?" he asked Mom.

"Sure," she said.

"I forgot all about this, but do you think this has anything to do with what I said at the conference?" he asked.

"Remind me, what did you say?" she asked.

He thought about it. "I said, 'Every kid should have her name on the board at least once in her life. Anyone who tries to be perfect is in for a rude awakening. It's the slip ups in life that build character, don't you think?' I meant it as an offhand comment, but you don't think she took me at my word, do you?" he asked Mom.

I happened to be standing at the door with my ear to the wall. My mind flashed back to seeing my name in all-capital letters, underlined, and the shame I had felt in thinking I had done something wrong. I stormed into the room, stomping my feet in a fit.

"You did what?" I yelled at Dad. "You've destined me to failure, a pathetic adult life on that sofa." I felt so betrayed, set up by my own flesh and blood. At first, I wallowed in self-pity, especially that Monday when I was in the cafeteria dodging Brandon's and Reagan's spit wads while the gold-star recipients engulfed greasy burgers and fries.

But then, one day, I let it go, just as simple as that. Even now, Dad and I tease each other about what we call "THE INCIDENT." Dad still likes to remind me that I learned a valuable lesson that day.

"Life's not fair," he says, wagging his pointer finger at me in satisfaction. And to this day, a piercing pang shoots through my blood when he says it, and we both laugh nervously, knowing that I truly believe that my permanent record sits, dotted with one tiny asterisk dating back to the sixth grade, in some abstract location in the great academic abyss.

HIDDEN PLAINS DANCES

Twice a year, Hidden Plains hosted coed, middle-school dances in the gymnasium. The lights would be low, and there would be boys. My friends and I needed new outfits to wear.

Mom took a group of us to a store at the mall known for its clothing geared toward teenagers. My friends and I were still 12, so it was very exciting to shop at a store that sold Pepe and Marithe et Francois Girbaud jeans, the must-have items of the 1990s.

After several outfit changes, I selected as my new outfit purple clogs, knee-high, striped socks, boot-cut Pepe jeans and a black T-shirt screen-printed with a yellow peace sign, an image of the earth and a famous lyric from the song "Imagine," written by John Lennon, a man whose name I never had heard.

Dances usually started with one big group of girls standing still on the left side of the gym and the boys pacing nervously on the right side of the gym. Our adult chaperones and teachers seemed to be more than happy to spy on us the entire evening. We figured it must have been their whole social life given the way they monitored the bathroom stalls with flashlights like detectives.

My grade level posed for a group photo, which turned out to be an explosion of mismatched, neon outfits showcasing 13 girls, some in straw hats with fake flowers pressed on the fronts and sides, others in "denim sandwiches," consisting of denim, button-down shirts and jeans of exactly the same shade. That was what happened when girls confined to uniforms tried to dress themselves on the weekends.

Once the peppy dance music kicked in over the loudspeaker, Julia Poppy, one of the two shyest girls in our grade, started freestyle dancing. She did the karate chop and the robot in the center of the circle, and no one could figure out what had brought on her energy. Maybe it was that all of the overhead lights were shut off, save for the three strobe lights that one of the teachers had rented.

The majority of the girls, myself included, were still sitting on the bleachers, waiting for this fiasco to be over. Then, to our utter shock, Tim Chamberlain, a fifth grader, walked into the gym with a group of, gasp, public-school girls, who marched up to the deejay and requested the inappropriate-for-middle-school-kids song, "C'mon 'N Ride It (The Train)."

The advanced public-school girls and our beloved, naive fifth-grade boys formed a human chain and started a combination of the moving limbo and a series of pelvic thrusts that made us private-school girls feel the need to cover our eyes. Soon enough, that nonsense was over, and a slow song boomed over the speakers.

I got major anxiety about slow songs, worrying whether some broken-out boy, certain to be shorter than me, would shuffle over and ask me to the dance floor, where I'd stand and awkwardly tower over him for three uninterrupted minutes. Even worse was the thought that no one would ask me to dance.

The slow song, "Heaven," by Nu Flavor, was one of my favorites. I owned the cassette tape, and Kristen Bennett and I listened to the song on repeat in my bedroom upstairs, imagining our future boyfriends serenading us outside my window.

Together, Kristen and I sat in the bleachers when two public-school boys walked in with Luke Griffin, Brent Dawson, Ben Teague and the rest of the seventh-grade boys whom all of the sixth-grade girls loved and adored.

I sat up a little straighter and said to Kristen, "I like the tall one." They looked over at us, and the tall one must have seen my hint of a smile that accompanied the display of hormonal fireworks that were going off inside my stomach.

He walked right up to me and said, "Hi, I'm Hunter. Want to dance?" as he extended his hand.

Chivalry lives, I thought. His shorter sidekick, the perfect height for petite Kristen, asked her to dance too.

Hunter and I swayed back and forth, our feet planted in the same places the entire time the song played. My knees would not bend, and my stiff arms began to ache as they remained extended toward his tall shoulders. Hunter tried to make small talk, but with the loud music and the fact that we were standing with an imaginary beach ball between us, we practically yelled to be understood. I was definitely paying more attention to his hands on my waist than to the conversation, though I did catch that he would be advancing the following year from seventh grade to eighth grade at his school.

So Hunter was older than me and went to public school, which made me wonder how Mom and Dad would feel once they found out. After all, I told my parents everything.

As the song ended, Hunter asked for my phone number. Oh no, I thought. He obviously wants to move forward, which might mean calling me every couple of nights and eventually inviting me to a movie matinee.

The nerves pumping through my body told me I wasn't ready for this. I could envision myself checking the caller ID and shutting off my answering machine whenever I saw Hunter's name appear. I wasn't sure that I was comfortable with the name Hunter, which made me feel a lot like Bambi's mother from the Disney film.

This was our conversation during "Heaven," which from that moment on, Hunter probably would remember as "our song."

"So what's your name?"

"Ashley."

"How old are you?"

"Twelve. You?"

"Fourteen."

"What's your favorite sports team?"

"The New York Knicks and the Chicago Bulls."

"Cool. So can I have your phone number?"

I hesitated. How could I worm my way out of this one?

"Umm, sure," I said. I wrote down my name and phone number, which was listed under "children's line" in the local phonebook, on the small, white business card he handed me. I turned over the card, and it gave his orthodontist's business info, including a short list of the options of numbing-solution flavors his patients could choose.

I looked up at Hunter, and he grinned. "Grape and strawberry are my favorites," he said, exposing a mouthful of braces and colorful rubber bands.

"Cool," I said.

The song ended, and I returned to my seat in the bleachers alongside Kristen. We exchanged a knowing look. Our social life consisted of playing on repeat Boyz II Men's "A Song for Mama," the undisputed tribute song about a mother's love.

Sure, Kristen and I were known to recline on the carpet in my bedroom and daydream about cute boys whisking us away to a future of dancing to romantic music in the kitchen as our kids watched cartoons over bowls of cereal. But in that moment, I had a revelation that I was much more comfortable with the dream of love than the reality.

I guess Kristen realized it too. "Wanna get out of here?" she asked.

I couldn't have been happier. "I'll call Mom from the pay phone to pick us up," I said.

As soon as we got home, I tossed my Nu Flavor cassette tape into the trash, and Kristen and I spent the rest of the evening listening to country-music infomercials, the ones with multiple albums compiled from the greatest songs of all time. We came up with a competition to see which one of us could remember faster the lyrics to each song as the titles ticked down the screen while a musician performed one featured selection in the background.

I flung off the purple clogs that had rubbed a blister on my toes, and we both changed to our long-sleeved Joe Boxer pajama tops and long, elastic-waisted pants that were perfect for next weekend's all-girls slumber party at Kristen's. My interest in boys would develop over time, but for now, I just wanted to be a 12-year-old girl who dreamed about Mom's homemade mashed potatoes and boys who would enter my life years down the road.

A NEW FRIEND

To say I was intimidated by the students in the grades above would be an understatement. Entertained, yes, but also very frightened. It all started with Tina Schumacher, two years older than Kristen Bennett and me but light years ahead in the race for pubescent progress. Tina's three trademarks were her stately square jaw, her blunt, cropped bangs and her husky voice.

Fortunately for Kristen and me, she only crossed our paths if she intended to talk to Emily Holland, whose parents were friends with Tina's parents. If Tina ever tried to make eye contact with me, I never knew it. I was too busy staring off blankly into the horizon, while Kristen preferred the view of the linoleum floor.

Two quick facts about Tina Schumacher. One: She had an undisputed starting position on the normally all-boys flag-football team. Two: Hidden Plains enforced a strict no gum-chewing, no peppermint-eating policy. Tina not only tucked peppermints between her teeth and cheeks as if sucking on wads of dip, but also discarded the plastic candy wrappers inside her desk at school. Teachers ground their upper and lower molars at the mere mention of her name. They practically scavenged for evidence to expel Tina from Hidden Plains.

Needless to say, Tina Schumacher was not part of my inner circle. That is, until she said otherwise. One day, Tina came hulking toward me down the hallway. When I did my usual stare to the left off into the distance, she scooted to the left, and the infinite horizon gave way to Tina, only a few centimeters away. I searched for an emergency escape route. With lockers lining either side, I had nowhere to go.

Because of her alpine stature, my eyes stared straight into her stomach. I shifted my gaze upward, arching my neck muscles.

"Hey," Tina said, her stony expression morphing into an awkward smile.

Here we go, I thought. Was Tina going soft before making me her afternoon snack? Would the newspaper team write an article after they found traces of my bones scattered across campus?

Tina continued, "Hey. You can say hi to me when I pass you in the hallway."

No words were worthy enough to express my instant relief, so I abided there, frozen in silence. "Okay?" she said almost pleadingly.

"Sure, Tina," I said. "Whatever you say."

Tina loaded her bulky textbooks into my arms, and I trailed

behind her, tagging along to her next class as my classmates pointed and chided. But I lugged the heavy books with pride, beaming a smile at my friends, sure that my newfound "hallway cred" was worth some extra baggage.

THE SHOELACE REBELLION

The chaos began when, in a blatant act of rebellion, Robin's classmate Summer Hodges wore neon-green shoelaces to school. Summer had spent hours scanning the Hidden Plains student handbook's dress code with the precision of a criminal defense attorney, only to find no mention whatsoever of stipulated shoelace colors.

Sure enough, the next day at school, the teachers' and administration members' eyes zoomed in like radars to Summer's green laces, and they told her she must discard them. She happened to have a copy of the Hidden Plains handbook with her, and with no written enforcement of their instruction, Summer had won the battle, rendering her superiors defenseless. She wore neon-green shoelaces throughout the remaining school days of that calendar year.

By day one of the following school year, the Hidden Plains

board of directors had written a new policy that read, "Students may wear red, white or blue shoelaces only. Aforementioned shoelaces are to be laced into red, white or blue shoes. Brown penny loafers are also allowed."

That's when Randy Pearson, an unruly seventh grader, took over the reins of rebellion from Summer. During Mrs. Bonham's computer class, he ventured off for a restroom break, where he tossed his tan penny loafers into the trashcan.

He then pulled two brown paper towels from the dispenser and "laced" his "shoes" by securing them with three red staples. Randy walked down the hallways and on the concrete courtyard, just waiting for a faculty member to see and reprimand him.

Soon enough, Randy caught sight of the sun's bright glare reflecting off Mr. Barry Wilson's bald head. Mr Wilson was the Hidden Plains discipline foreman who roamed the campus in search of someone to write up for detention. Small groups from every grade crowded into the courtyard to witness what we hoped would be the ultimate duel of words.

"Take off your shoes, I mean paper towels, young man," Mr. Wilson said. "They do not meet the dress code."

"Actually, they do," Randy said. "These are my brown loafers."

"They may be brown, but paper towels aren't loafers," Mr. Wilson said.

"But I am a loafer, and as a part of me, my shoes are by association," Randy said. "And as you know, sir, brown loafers are permitted as per the Hidden Plains dress code, section 25, paragraph two."

The sun gleamed brighter off of Mr. Wilson's now red-as-Mars forehead. And so Randy wore paper towels and rotated red, white and blue staples each day throughout the rest of the school year.

Meanwhile, the Hidden Plains faculty and administration members combined forces with the board of directors to clarify the student handbook's dress code yet again. The final version read, "Students must wear red, white or blue shoelaces only, comprised of durable materials such as cotton or nylon (no staples), which are to be laced into red, white or blue shoes. Brown penny loafers (leather only) are allowed. All shoes must be made of durable materials, and soles must measure at least half-an-inch thick (no paper towels)."

The final dress code read like a legal love letter, personalized and continually updated for inventive students like Summer Hodges and Randy Pearson.

GONE WITH THE HIDDEN PLAINS OF TEXAS WIND

One day, I looked out the window in Mzzz T's biology class to find Robin and some of her classmates chasing the wind for sheets of notebook paper, which quickly scattered across the brown field. I motioned to Mzzz T and my classmates to come join me in watching the commotion.

Mzzz T wiggled out of her adjustable chair cushion, which sprang up five inches when she left her position to waddle to the window. Known best for the feisty temper that turned her entire face bright pink, save for one permanently white square patch on her neck, Mzzz T must have developed a sudden, temporary case of empathy for my sister and her classmates.

"Poor babies," Mzzz T said as she saw 12 of them scramble to grasp the air for their lost homework. "They're probably worried sick that they'll get in trouble for being tardy to

English. I'll go tell Mrs. Davies that they'll be a few minutes late and not to reprimand them."

"Bless their hearts," she continued on her way out the door. "We'd all be frantic if the powerful Texas wind gobbled up our essays on Fyodor Dostoevsky."

She waddled down the hall to alert Mrs. Bonham and Mr. Llewellyn en route to Mrs. Joyce Davies' room at the end of the hall. The rest of us stood by the window, laughing, pointing and hoping we would get to watch them run clear across the field to gather the product of all their hard work at home.

And that's when it happened. First, Chris Butler pulled from his backpack a package of brand-new, blank notebook paper. Robin did the same, then Faith Sharp and Bethany Simmons, and so on. Together, in an act of defiant solidarity, they ripped the clear plastic coating from the packages and tossed 500 pieces of blank, lined, triple-hole-punched notebook paper into the dirt-laced Texas wind.

There in Mzzz T's biology room we stood, dumbfounded and impressed at their ability to devise such an unassuming scheme to skip the most rigorous English class in Hidden Plains history.

Unfortunately for them, Mzzz T toddled back into her science room at that exact moment. Anger shadowed her otherwise sunny, round face until its mass was bright red, except for the white, square patch in the middle of her neck, which never changed color.

"Oh," she breathed calmly, a sure sign of the calm before the storm. "I see we've been hoodwinked by some of our older students." And she marched to the administration building, also known as "The Slammer," with a fistful of pink slips.

Just as we heard her short legs stalk back into the room,

Paul Townsend chose the most inopportune moment to verbalize his mental blueprint for a copycat act of rebellion.

"I think our class could totally get away with something similar," he said. "We're smarter, not to mention a lot less obvious than the older grades."

This time, Mzzz T's face morphed like a mood ring into the rarely seen shades of cobalt blue and indigo. I saw her jaw muscles clench her mouth completely shut. My mind's eye envisioned her as a warden, locking Paul into a jail cell as the bars closed in tightly around his freedom.

So, mostly out of fear, I blurted, "What a silly idea, Paul. We should...we should...offer to help clean up the mess they've made in the field." And though that too was a scheme of sorts, it had the same effect as sticking a pacifier into Mzzz T's mouth.

Her face came down to a less frightening, more gentle shade of red, and she marched us, a row of innocent felons with sharp-edged farming utensils, toward the dusty field, where we collected more than 2,000 sheets of blank, lined, triple-hole-punched notebook paper with not a mention of Fyodor Dostoevsky anywhere in sight.

During my entire tenure as a student, only once did I have a teacher whose clothing made as much noise as she did. Fiona Decker coached volleyball at Hidden Plains. During school hours, she wore the unofficial outfit of seemingly every school coach, a wind suit. Coach Decker's windbreaker jacket was mostly blue with red-and-white sections running across it diagonally. Her sweatpants were solid-blue nylon, and we could hear them go, "swish, swish," down the hall as her heavily endowed thighs rubbed together with every move.

Coach Decker was sturdy and, in my opinion, intimidating. The sound of her sweatsuit gave us that critical 10-second window to scrounge to our proper places before she arrived in the gym. It wasn't so much her words that made her intense but her overall demeanor.

Once, she corrected Becca Stafford on her volleyball stance

without even raising her voice. But Coach Decker's icy body language and steely stare down were enough to send Becca running down the long hall to cry in the girls' restroom. In a wave of compassion, the rest of us trailed after her like a row of baby duckings.

Coach Decker had big, gaping eyes, and she lined her top and bottom lashes with heavy mascara. She painted a thick, blue stripe of eyeliner on her top lids. Chandelier earrings always dangled from her earlobes, causing a long hole that stretched down the entire lobe.

During practice, Coach Decker taught us how to bump, set and spike the volleyball, but her favorite activity was serving the ball. Though my teammates and I were far too weak for anything but an underhand serve, Coach Decker tried to make us masters of the powerful overhead serve, which she delighted in demonstrating to us.

First, she bounced the ball several times. Then, she threw the ball over her head and slammed it with her palm, catapulting it across the net as if she were slapping the poor volleyball in the face. Her bleached-blonde ponytail, which she secured on the right side of her head with a red, white and blue bow of ribbons wrapped over a rubber band, didn't move a millimeter, thanks to her liberally applied aerosol hairspray. The tighter the ponytail, the more her eyes bulged, and the more her dark roots seemed to peek forth above her tightly curled bangs.

Whenever Coach Decker served the ball, I dreaded being in the backcourt position, where I knew it was sure to land. My worst fear was that the combination of Coach Decker's aggressive serve and the ball's raging velocity would decapitate me.

I watched the ball fly across the net toward my face, and I imagined the impact would compare to a speeding pigeon headed straight for the windshield. In true wimp fashion, I dove belly down to the floor like I was seeking shelter during tornado season. The ball went splat and collided with the ground.

It was a bad break for me that Coach Decker won that point and seized the opportunity to serve again. This time, all of my teammates swayed left to right, and with animal instinct, Coach Decker detected our fear.

She hit the ball even harder than before and sent it sailing far over our heads until finally it slammed against the back wall, unhinging the plastic, padded mat that hung there just in case a hustling player collided with the wall. The mat was situated 10 feet past the out-of-bounds line, and I remember thinking, "If that's what it did to the mat, what would it have done to my head?"

That's when we realized that Coach Decker broke one of her fake nails on the serve. In reaction, she stared at those of us across the court and said, "Well...bless...your...hearts." By her tone and the saliva that flew with each elongated syllable, I could tell that Coach Decker now considered us not the opponent, but the enemy.

Believe it or not, Coach Decker had a doting husband, Dudley Decker. He was about half her size and had silver hair. Dudley followed Fiona everywhere, though that job description was nothing to boast about. Hidden Plains parents would see them at the pharmacy, Coach Decker looking through the candy aisle while Dudley fetched other items.

This royal attention earned her the nickname, "Lady Fi," and the Hidden Plains dads joked that Dudley should send his wife a "cease-and-Du-sist" letter. But instead, Dudley sat loyally on the sidelines, clapping fervently for the volleyball team.

Coach Decker said she would retire at the end of the school year. Her final mission with us was to serve as our jump-rope counselor for a middle-school competition to benefit a national charity. The students who jumped rope the longest in a timed race would win one of several prizes.

As always, Coach Decker demonstrated the proper form for us, though this time she wielded a jump rope. We marveled in a dumbfounded kind of way as she jumped for us, her thighs causing her sweatpants to go "swish, swish," her sizable breasts swinging up and down from her waist to her chin.

And after the competition came to a close, she kept her word and retired, vowing one final promise. "This time next year, you girls won't recognize me," she said with pride. "I'm going to be skinny enough to fit into a bikini, and Dudley and I are goin' to Aruba with the beautiful people." She showed us a faded, wallet-sized photo of a gorgeous, fit blonde.

"Whoa, who's the hottie?" Brandon Prescott II asked.

"That's me, 20 years ago," she said.

I could tell by Brandon's guttural reaction that he immediately regretted his comment. I thought he might regurgitate his Sloppy Joe sandwich right then and there.

Two years later, Mom and I went in a pharmacy, and as I waited for her in one of the plastic chairs, I heard a familiar sound that belonged only to Coach Decker.

Swish, swish, swish, swish. I looked up in terror and jumped out of the chair.

I followed the sound to Aisle 5 and stood at the end of the aisle, making sure the distance was safe enough that she couldn't see me but close enough that I could see her. There she was, Lady Fi, in sweatpants splendor, her thighs brushing against the patriotic colors of the nylon. A shopping basket hung like an oversized purse on her left forearm, and her eyes bulged as she glanced left and right, reaching out to pluck multiple boxes of Jolly Ranchers and Hot Tamales, which she dropped into her basket gracefully, just like a royal.

GIRLS JUST WANT TO HAVE FUN

One year, Nikki Spencer chose to have her birthday party at the mock recording studio inside Hidden Plains Mall. For the bargain rate of several-hundred dollars, the studio offered up the chance for us to be the Spice Girls or Shania Twain for the day.

When it came to celebrations, especially birthdays, the Spencers spared no expense, and so they rented out the whole studio for Nikki and her friends. There, a dozen preteen girls recorded our favorite songs in the soundproof recording booths, wearing giant, padded headphones and all.

Our vocal coaches divided us into four groups of three. Somehow, I ended up in a group with Maya Heinrich and Misty Gibson, both of whom I barely knew. It was safe to say none of us was a singing sensation.

For our song, Maya, Misty and I selected Cyndi Lauper's

"Girls Just Want To Have Fun." I liked the song and was pretty excited, I thought, until I saw the enthusiasm of Nikki, Emily Holland and Jasmine Pine, who finished recording their song just before my group was set to go. They were jamming out like the girl group Wilson Phillips. Nikki held one earphone against her right ear to simultaneously gauge her vocal range on tape and out loud. Emily closed her eyes, leaning into the microphone as if it were her closest confidante. Jasmine's voice boomed out, overshadowing everyone when she decided to become lead vocalist. It was just like when she played point guard for our basketball team and dribbled straight toward the basket to shoot.

Now, my group was up. I heard Cyndi Lauper's voice come through the airwaves. I tried to sing the lyrics, but the words I produced were muffled mumbles. The next three minutes proved that Misty was tone deaf, but she belted her heart out with reckless abandon. Maya opted to speak the lyrics rather than sing them. The result of our collaboration was a cacophonous massacre.

To kick us when we were down, the recording studio gave each group a parting gift, a cassette recording of our songs. Call it the party favor from hell. At least I could toss my tape in the trash and put this experience to permanent rest.

Then, Monday morning at school, Nikki pulled out a plastic bag full of cassette tapes during math class. For some reason, Mrs. Bonnie Clayton agreed to play all four group recordings for the entire class, including the boys.

Nikki, Emily and Jasmine, the Wilson Phillips trio, received mostly positive responses from their wholehearted version of "Hold On." I scanned my brain for an excuse to leave the room when I knew it was time to hear our song. But before I could ask Mrs. Clayton for a restroom break, she popped in our tape.

The melody started to play in the background, but there were no voices. Until, that is, we all heard what sounded like a whimpering cat, which was my contribution. That noise was followed by Misty's voice, which sounded like screeching brakes killing the whimpering cat. Maya's monotone speaking voice peeked through the background.

My stomach was in knots, and I was sure Brandon would humiliate me with some cutting remark. All he said was, "What song was that anyway?"

Everyone else looked straight ahead with eyes as enlarged and round as silver dollars. Even Mrs. Clayton, who always had something complimentary to say about her students, seemed at a loss this time. She remained dead silent while she replaced our cassette tape with the next group's.

It was in that moment that my no-hit wonder singing career slammed to a grinding halt. I remember thinking, "I'm going to be a writer someday. It may be the only profession where you get to work alone and don't have to speak or sing."

GONE FISHING

My dad was the father of two girls, and I always felt that he yearned for the companionship of a boy to wrestle with, shoot baskets with and take trout fishing. I could never be a boy, but I could be the closest thing a girl could be, a tomboy.

Kristen Bennett's dad Dave didn't have a boy either. So when our dads got the idea to take a father-daughter fishing trip deep in the Ozark mountains of Arkansas, Kristen and I, two gangly girls in neon Umbro wind shorts, happily signed on to accompany them on the journey.

Dave owned a used-car sales-and-rental business. He came home most evenings with a different ride, better described as a contraption. We got a huge kick out of the Chevy with no interior, which had rods for seats with no cushioning whatsoever. If Dave borrowed one of the trucks with no rear cab, Kristen and I wondered where we would sit during the 12-hour drive, knowing it would be an arduous trip.

But this time, Dave really came through for us. He selected an industrial-looking van that was very bare bones and upon first impression an old, giant rectangle with seats, but Kristen and I, being girls and amateur interior designers, viewed its potential, knowing we would thrive, not survive, a week in our home on wheels.

Kristen and I prepared for the trip by dividing and conquering the necessary tasks. I was in charge of the music, and I placed sticky notes on the CDs I wanted to take. Lisa Loeb's hit song, "Stay (I Missed You,)" was worth listening to over and over again, so we did. Ace of Base, Mariah Carey, Whitney Houston and Seal rounded out the lineup.

Kristen was in charge of redecorating the van's interior, a nonnegotiable clause in our verbal agreement with Dad and Dave. As long as we didn't do any irreversible damage, they were happy. As long as we could hang the family quilts as wallpaper and tape our printed computer signs that read "Ashley's shoes" and "Kristen's shoes" with designating arrows underneath, Kristen and I were happy.

And so the trek to Arkansas began. Dad and Dave sat in the front cabin and listened to political talk the entire 12 hours, working in stories about their childhoods and political views, neither of which interested Kristen and me at the time. To blot out the sounds of their voices and the radio rants, Kristen and I partitioned a blanket between them and us, which for all intents and purposes served as a surrogate wall. Unfortunately, the speakers were in the back of the van, so Dad and Dave cranked up the volume even louder than before.

Kristen and I subdivided our part of the van in half. We

spread quilts and blankets along the ground and truly felt that, if only our moms and my sister were there, we would be conquering America as family and friends in our covered wagon.

Eventually, we stopped to eat dinner and were astounded that Dad and Dave managed to find a healthy cafeteria in what seemed like the middle of nowhere. Kristen and I begged them to let us order food from the Burger King drive thru, and I was shocked that my own flesh and blood, whom I always counted on to be the more lenient of my parents, said, "I think you girls need to eat healthy food this evening. Sue and Mom have entrusted you to us this week, and we've got plenty of meals ahead of us."

We sulked until Dave started to cave and agreed to let us have chicken fingers and fries, just this once. Before that moment, Dave and Dad ranked dead even in the coolness department. Dave, who traveled long distances to drive back cars to resell, always brought back a surprise, which ranged from gummy penguin candy to collectible pet rocks, for Kristen and me. Dad, meanwhile, took us on Sundays to the furniture store when it was closed to customers and let us jump across the rows of display mattresses, squealing as loudly as our lungs would allow.

In a fine display of maturity, I said to Dad, "Obviously Dave is going to be the cool father on this trip." Well, that sealed the deal, and Kristen and I were stuck at a table for four eating green beans and steamed spinach as we gave our dads the silent treatment.

A few hours later, we arrived in the mountains of Arkansas. Dave and Dad told us to pull down the window quilts and look at some of the most beautiful scenery God had created.

As our van weaved on the road right next to the bluest, purest water we'd ever seen, Kristen and I got pretty excited about the upcoming days of adventure. It was the kind of place where you could get lost, and we planned to do just that.

The first order of business was to pitch two tents about 30 yards from the riverbank. We let our dads do all of the heavy lifting, of course. There we met our guides for the week, a group of four guys who would take us to the best fishing spots and cook our meals for us each evening.

Believe it or not, Kristen and I couldn't have been more excited about sleeping on cots. That first night before bedtime, we crowded into one tent with Dave and Dad, where Dave told us stories about his humble beginnings in rural Indiana, where he walked a mile to school with no shoes in the snow, a story every person over 40 seemed to want to share with members of the younger generation.

"Hey, does your dad snore?" I asked Kristen.

"I think so," she said.

"Mine too," I said.

Though the sleeping arrangements were supposed to be one father and one daughter to a tent, we negotiated a trade, making them sleep in the other tent, where we figured they would drown each other out with their snoring.

Early the next morning, Kristen and I hiked up the mountain to locate the outhouse. We heard some rustling in the bushes and discovered a stray golden retriever whom we named Alfie and nicknamed Alfie Alfredo. We used an entire roll of disposable camera film snapping photos of him, and we promised we would come back and adopt him someday.

That day, we sat on the boat and fished for hours upon hours, our main source of excitement being the live crawfish our guides used as bait. Each time the guides removed a crawfish from the tackle box, Kristen and I screamed and leapt with bare feet to the back of the boat until it was safely fastened onto our fishing rod.

We could not wait to return to camp, where Leroy, the cook, prepared our dinner. Over an open fire, he deep fried our catches in a large pan and produced the tastiest trout, crunchiest potatoes and creamiest refried beans I'd ever tasted.

Leroy wore overalls and spoke with a thick drawl. I remember him as one of the gentlest, kindest men I had ever met, and as he tossed around the items in his frying pan, he told us the greatest, most embellished tall tales I had ever heard.

"This beats the Burger King drive thru any day of the week," I said to Dad as I scarfed down my crispy, brown fish and greasy potatoes.

"I told you there would be plenty of meals ahead of us," he said, smiling.

The next day, we left right after dawn for a full morning of fishing. As the rest of us motored away in our two boats, Leroy waved at us from the comfort of his plastic lawn chair.

Kristen and I thought we were in paradise, whipping through the crisp water in one boat with our dads in another boat a few feet away. A couple of hours later, our guides decided to have a little fun.

"You girls want to challenge your dads to a fishing contest?" one of them asked us.

"Sure," we said, agreeing to reconvene at camp three hours later for lunch and to see who had won the contest.

Our guide zoomed us in the motorboat to what turned out to be just the right spot for biting trout. They used the priciest bait from the fishing pro shop, and Kristen and I reeled in five fish for every one Dad and Dave caught in a not-too-distant part of the river. As we giggled with contentment, we could see our dads shaking their heads as they realized--a major clue being the chuckling guides in both boats--that our friendly little fishing contest was rigged.

Dad told me later, "I was afraid you're going to think fishing will always be that easy."

The four of us ate fried trout, greasy potatoes and refried beans for one week solid, served up on our trays courtesy of Leroy, whose delicious food had Kristen and me convinced he was the Wolfgang Puck of the great outdoors.

During our last meal together on the final night of our trip, Dad, Dave, Kristen and I sat around the campfire with Leroy and our guides when the conversation turned serious. The locals who had served us well the past week started to tell us about their health woes. Kristen and I heard a lot of new terms like high cholesterol, high blood pressure, hardened plaque and clogged arteries.

Leroy mentioned that he was about to have quadruple-bypass heart surgery, and the other guides said they'd all had at least three or four open-heart surgeries.

"I tell you, it's the biggest mystery," Leroy said, tugging on his baseball cap. "There must be something in the water here is all I can figure."

The guides stared at the open flame and nodded their heads in agreement. By the looks on their faces, the four of us could tell they were dead serious.

I looked down at the diced potatoes in the middle of my tray, now dripping excess oil out toward the edges. My crispy, brown entree was unrecognizable as trout. And the refried beans? Well, given their name, I figured they had been fried at least twice.

Suddenly, my appetite vanished into the clean mountain air, and I caught Dad's glance from across the campfire. The caring way he smiled and the sheepish way I smiled told me that we were thinking the same thing.

I still wonder whether I actually thanked him for the number of years he added to my adult life by forcing Kristen and me to eat all those vegetables that I mistakenly thought were brown and crusted, not green and leafy, in their natural state.

Madame Claudia Bissette was our middle-school French teacher, known to us simply as "Madame." As kids, we had no idea that "Madame" translated simply to "Mrs." and that each time we addressed her, we were saying things like, "Good morning, Mrs." and "This vocabulary lesson sure was hard, Mrs.," but in French.

Every title sounded romantic and appropriate in French. Madame certainly liked that nickname better than "Sadaam," the one the junior-high students had given her because it rhymed with the Iraqi dictator's name. They held a grudge after the eighth-grade trip to France, when she roamed the hotel halls, placing a stick of tape between each outside door and its frame to ensure no students snuck out to party at the Parisian discos. The next morning, she scanned the doors again, searching for pieces of broken tape with her magnifying glass.

Madame was a refined lady who barely spoke above a whisper. My mom determined that Madame's soft-spoken nature was a signal that I should sit on the front row, lean forward as she spoke, gather information audible only to hearing-trained dogs, earn good grades and so on.

At the time, Madame seemed elderly, as many teachers seem to young students. But 20 years later she was still alive, so we figured she had been middle-aged and just about the only teacher who didn't dye her hair. Until the day she showed up with lightly tinted, purple hair, which was the same day I regretted my choice of a front-row seat.

I had never mastered the art of withholding laughter at inopportune moments. The entire class had the giggles, but I kept quiet until finally the hysteria erupted through both my nostrils.

My sister and her classmates told us that Madame always kept a drawer of candy, or les bonbons en francais, in her desk drawer in case she needed to inspire our French memorization skills. But Robin and her friends warned us that Madame's offer came with one strict stipulation. "You must ask her, 'Do you have some candy, please?' in French," they said.

We had to bribe them with loose change in exchange for the translation, but a school-day sugar rush was worth every penny.

The next day, Kristen Bennett, Becca Stafford and I skipped into the classroom and smiled sweetly at Madame. We batted our eyelashes as frequently as possible and asked in unison, "Est-ce que vous avez des bonbons, s'il vous plait?"

Madame threw her head back and laughed heartily. She

unlocked her bottom desk drawer and divulged dozens of crunchy-on-the-outside, chewy-on-the-inside, cream-filled candies tied at both ends in golden wrappers.

To us, she looked like Mother Ginger in *The Nutcracker*, unloading from her drawers a multitude of little delights that scampered eagerly toward us for consumption. If we continued to charm Madame at this rate, our small frames would increase by an exponent of three toward the end of the year.

Madame was a native French speaker, born in Paris in the 1930s. French, to her, was the mother tongue. To her Texan students, far removed from any region where the language of culture was spoken, it was the refined and regal but distant great aunt we rarely saw. So when we needed methods to learn whether to use "etre," meaning "to be," or "avoir," meaning "to have," as helping verbs, Madame said, "You just have to memorize them."

We privately took a poll and decided to give up learning the language and instead focus on the culture. We had big plans for class parties where we would all bring different flavors of French cheeses and bonbons.

Madame hosted elaborate parties in her classroom, and her students brought decadent French cheeses. Our moms escorted us to the gourmet section of the grocery store in search of brie and camembert, delighted that their epicurean children had taken such an active interest in French class.

My favorite purchase was the bright-yellow cheese within the red, circular plastic shell that unraveled gracefully. Mom said a silent prayer, thankful that I had switched to a cheese that was somewhat healthier than artificially yellow, processed cheese.

Madame taught us to polka, and every two days she would

play a cassette of French tunes and coach les garcons on how to ask les femmes to dance. Perched on her desk, Madame smiled as the young gentlemen extended their right feet, offered us their hands and asked, "Est-ce que vous voulez danser avec moi?"

"How romantic," we said, swooning as they twirled us around the carpeted classroom floor. Madame's chivalry coaching service for boys set our expectations high for the years of dating that were to follow.

Robin and her friends hinted to us that Madame would veer off topic when asked about WWII. So when she said, "Today we will discuss le futur imparfait et le subjunctive. Open your books to Chapter Seven," we responded, "Oh, but Madame, will you tell us about the war?"

She whisked us into WWII Paris, where she and her sister had been frightened by Nazi guards on their bicycles before the family emigrated to the United States. She showed us her French passport from the 1950s that she kept in her top desk drawer. The black-and-white photo revealed a radiant, young beauty with wavy, brown hair and heavy, red lipstick that appeared much darker in print.

The foreign passport seemed like an ancient artifact worthy of a museum like the Smithsonian. We never had imagined that our teacher could have been so stunning and so close to our current ages. We had her stuck in time as elderly with purple hair.

Madame was pleased by our interest in her stories and continued to store the document in her desk drawer as an easily accessible reference point. That moment of camaraderie marked an important watermark in our journey through France.

Most of us never achieved francophone status, but thanks to Madame's class, the ennui of our textbooks was replaced by the joie de vivre of her recollections, and we embarked on a lifelong mission to explore French culture and let the language of love romance our souls.

THE HAIRCUT

During the 1990s, it seemed like every mother of every adolescent daughter wanted her to be refined, proper and above all, a "lady," emanating a demure yet confident air. I guess that's why Mom signed me up for refinement classes at Wilfred Brenhoffer Modeling Agency.

Judging by its low-budget ads on TV, in which a twangy female voiceover boasted about one of their students going to "New Yark Seaty," this was a local, I repeat local, modeling agency of the rudimentary kind.

Judith Dillard taught Refinement 101 every Thursday at 5 p.m. sharp. Wilfred Brenhoffer never made an appearance, and we have yet to figure out exactly where or who he was. Maybe he was the one graduate who made it to New York City.

Judith, a middle-aged woman characterized by her heavily padded business suits and ability to elongate one syllable into three, was considered to be extremely advanced for that time in her use of technology.

One of the agency's rooms featured a rinky-dink catwalk, standing only four inches off the ground, covered in green shag carpet. It was here where Judith instructed us to sashay and swing our hips while she stood in front of us with a handheld camcorder. When we reached the end of the catwalk, we had to stop, one foot extended outward and one hand on our hip, and say, "Hello, my name is Ashley Vaughn, and I am a student at the Wilfred Brenhoffer Modeling Agency."

Kristen Bennett was the only other student, so we struggled to get through it without bursts of laughter at Judith's expense. Minutes later, Judith plugged a cord into the 24-inch TV she wheeled in on a gurney and critiqued our posture and enunciation. The whole thing made an already awkward life stage all the more awkward.

After that, it was time for Judith's beauty school. She handed us each a single sheet of paper that listed various brands of face wash whose names sounded more like nasty skin diseases than solutions for acne.

"Ashley, what kind of soap do you use on your face?" Judith asked.

I honestly didn't know how to answer her question. "I use bar soap," I said.

Judith gasped. "You mean you use the same kind of soap on your face and your armpits?" she asked.

"I hadn't thought of it that way, but I guess," I said.

Judith laughed, no, cackled. "Well, it's a wonder you don't have breakouts all over your face," she said.

I swear, she emphasized the words "all over," implying that part of my face already looked like a pepperoni pizza.

That was it. I'd had enough. When I saw Mom's tires in the parking lot, I stormed outside and slammed the passenger door. Before she could say "peep," I told Mom why I no longer wanted to attend classes, even though Kristen was there with me. I repeated what Judith had said, that she had mocked my breakouts, that she was surprised they weren't "all over" my pizza face. If Mom thought she could just buy me off with some product that said "for facial use only," she was wrong.

I was never going back through the doors of Wilfred Brenhoffer's agency. I had my pride.

Until the following week, when Mom dropped off Kristen and me and told us she would be back in two hours. I wasn't happy about this, so I purposely flung open the agency's double doors without even looking back to see whether anyone was coming in behind me. So much for holding doors and all the other etiquette hoopla, I thought in a huff.

"Today we will discuss hairstyles, and which ones best suit the shape of our faces," Judith said. She suggested that we look through fashion magazines for styles we liked. Then, she said something that caught my attention.

"During next week's class, we will be visiting Mitchell's Hair Palace to get our hair cut. Any type of cut you want, Mitch will do," she said.

Suddenly, this lady was speaking my language. The salon owner, Mitch, short for Mitchell, was Mom's hair stylist. He was a small man with big dreams for his clients' hair. Mom was prone to calling Mitch "scissor happy" because when she told him she wanted a trim, he got a little spastic and took off at least four inches.

For his part, Dad enjoyed ribbing Mom about her expensive taste in haircuts.

"Well, Mitch charges so much, he's just trying to give you more for your money," Dad explained. "Unfortunately for you," he added, "The more you pay, the more you lose. Hair, that is."

I knew Mom would not be pleased with Judith's idea of letting us choose our own hairstyles, so for the first time ever, I kept a secret from Mom. I had long hair my whole life. Mom never allowed me to cut it short, so the thought of watching huge chunks of it fall to the floor made my mouth water in anticipation.

One of my female classmates, Holly Gallagher, had gotten a haircut, and she looked like a boy. Her mom decided Holly's hair took too much time and effort to style, so off it went, sheared at the neck with sideburns, just like a boy. I didn't want to go to that extreme, but the small rebellious streak within me caused my heart to flutter at the thought of being the anti-debutante.

For the next week, I played along and feigned happiness about Thursday's session. Meanwhile, I was storing up clips of models in my beauty binder. Only pixie cuts and styles cropped above the chin went into my collection.

Finally, haircut day had arrived, and Mom dropped us at Wilfred Brenhoffer. "Have fun," she said, very confused by my sudden change in attitude.

"Oh, I will," I thought. "I really will." Take a good look because the next time you see me, I'll have the Holly G. cut. I gave Mom the pageant wave and a huge grin before running inside.

We set out for Mitchell's Hair Palace in Judith's sedan. The salon was a sea of green walls accented with purple swirls and translucent, plastic partitions dividing each stylist's station. Above the shampooing sinks were mirrored ceilings so clients could look on as stylists washed and detangled their hair with a comb.

At the entry counter was a framed photo of Miss Hidden Plains. It was implied that Mitch was an official hairdresser for the Miss Texas pageant. He had some sort of verbal agreement to travel to Dallas to fix Miss Hidden Plains' hair most every year, so in a roundabout way his claim was valid. In any case, it garnered him a lot of local business among big-haired women, so Mitch was laughing all the way to the bank.

Kristen was up first for the cut of her choice. Her hair was already pretty short, so she decided on a simple trim. Mitch's scissors looked a little melancholy as far as I was concerned. Boring. I hoped they'd be scissor happy by the time my seat reached the chair.

As I watched Kristen get her trim, I thought about the times when my mom got a cut. Her back was to the mirror, so when Mitch whirled her rotating chair around, she looked in the mirror with huge eyes. Then, she stared at the ground, where Mitch had lopped off at least four inches. She and her locks were so close, yet so far away.

But Mom never said anything, like, "What have you done?" She simply thanked Mitch, proceeded to the register and paid the bill. And without fail she scheduled her next appointment for eight weeks from that exact date.

She walked back to Mitch's section and placed a twice-folded $10 bill on the counter next to his styling chair, where another customer was directing Mitch about her wishes for her cut. He never seemed to take notes on paper or in his mind.

Once we were inside the car, she pulled down the front-seat mirror and launched into a five-minute spiel about Mitch's blinded excitement when his shears met her split ends. I couldn't understand the vicious cycle of her continual return.

But, hey, Mitch had styled Miss Hidden Plains' hair for the statewide pageant.

"Your turn, Ashley," Judith said as Kristen stepped forward from the chair. I handed Mitch the magazine photo I had selected.

"You're your mama's daughter," he said. "You like it short."

Mitch prepared for his performance. As he closed his eyes and elevated his shoulders, I caught his vision. My wet hair was his blank canvas, and Mitch was about to slather sections of it onto my smock like Jackson Pollock splashed reds and blues and greens with his brush. Mom would ground me for weeks, but it was going to be worth it.

And then it happened. In the foreground, I could see Mitch's sharp scissors within an inch of my ends. A squawking, flapping figure swooped in through the background, screaming in what seemed like slow motion, "Wait!...No!...Stop!"

It was Mom, who apparently had come to save my hair and shred my dignity. In one swift motion, she flung herself from the elevated register area to the styling floor, skipping all three stairs in her wholehearted display of martyrdom.

She had clued in to my ploy when she noticed that the day's pick-up location was at Mitchell's Hair Palace. Call it maternal instinct, but she knew I was up to something. In a single instant, Mom foiled weeks of my scheming and false pleasantness about going to Wilfred Brenhoffer.

She put her arm around my shoulders and escorted me to the car. She wasn't mad, she was relieved. I was the one who was steaming, at her of course for rescuing my hair.

"I just don't know what we'd have done if I hadn't come in

before it was too late," she said. "Your hair has always been so long and beautiful." And then she looked at me, paused, and asked ever so sweetly, "Honey, why would you want your hair cut like a little boy?"

I placed my hand on her shoulder and said, "I don't want to look like a boy, Mom. But I absolutely despise refinement class, and I'm about to crater under Judith's idea of a lady."

Right then and there, Mom and I made a pact. I'd lose the idea to chop off my hair, and she'd agree to let me drop out of beauty school. We celebrated my freedom with a mother-daughter date of two glazed donuts and six vanilla donut holes.

And just like Mom's triumphant entry into Mitchell's Hair Palace, our agreement couldn't have come at a more opportune time. Judith's topic for the next week was slated to be "Angling Your Chin to Look Thin in a Photo."

SLUMBER PARTIES

One Friday afternoon, during a typically uninspiring basketball practice, I was busy anticipating the slumber party I was set to host at our house later that evening. Ninety-five percent of our middle-school basketball team endured practices by yawning and fanning ourselves. Only Becca Stafford and Jasmine Pine exhibited any form of competitiveness, which was probably why they armored their bodies with elbow pads and protective goggles.

Becca proved to be particularly feisty that day, shaking her jowls like a dog taking out its aggression on a squeaky chew toy. Coach Hobbs divided us into two teams of five each for a scrimmage, and Holly Gallagher drew the shortest straw, so to speak, when Coach assigned her to guard Becca.

Becca darted to and from the basket to chase down rebounds. I think Coach was trying to reward her hustle because suddenly he called a shooting foul on Holly, whose defensive energy matched that of Winnie the Pooh's lethargic friend Eeyore the donkey.

Becca stood at the line and sent her inner dynamite into the ball, which bricked off the backboard with a loud thud. Her second-and-final shot slammed off the backboard like the first, but this time Becca lurched over the line and miraculously caught her own rebound. Becca had deemed the ball hers.

When Holly stepped over to guard her, Becca seemed to grow octopus tentacles, judging from the way she threw out her elbows to secure one measly rebound that wasn't of lasting consequence in our little scrimmage. Time stood still as I watched in slow motion Becca's elbow collide with Holly's left eye. Becca gasped in horror, but Holly stood there, emotionless.

Kristen Bennett and I darted to the cafeteria kitchen for ice, and practice jolted to an abrupt end 30 minutes early, which was bitter yet sweet, since I did have to prepare for that night's slumber party.

Fast forward a few hours to when my guests began arriving at our house. First was Kristen, since she lived on the block, then Elise Rousseau, then a humble and contrite Becca, followed by Jasmine and several others who rang the doorbell as a group.

Right after we dug into the birthday cake, Holly showed up, which created a stunned, awkward silence among my company. But, after all, this was an all-girls slumber party, so it's not like we were just going to sit around in silence. There were pizzas to be eaten and catfights to be started.

At any given time period during the school year, two girls were at odds. That year, it was Jasmine and Elise. Knowing full well that Elise never had learned to swim, Jasmine swam to the edge of the deep end of the pool.

With the empty promise of extending the olive branch, Jasmine lured Elise to the edge of the deep end, where she stood just outside the pool with a slice of pizza in her hand. When Jasmine's and Elise's palms met for a truce, Jasmine gripped Elise's wrist and twisted it, sending Elise and her slice of pizza splashing 13 feet below, toward the drain at the bottom of the pool.

Five of us dove over like synchronized-swimming life savers and paddled Elise to shore. To her credit, Jasmine handed Elise a pool towel as Elise climbed the four rungs of the pool ladder in the deep end. The majority of the group sided with Elise, but out of obligation two girls sided with Jasmine.

We spent the rest of the slumber party running up and down the stairs to film the two factions. The impartial cameraperson acted as a gopher, running from the upstairs bedroom, where Jasmine's group held camp, to the downstairs bathroom, where Elise's faction barricaded themselves.

We conducted interviews that I'm sure caused my parents guilt and horror years later when they watched the tapes expecting family memories from Walt Disney World and instead found footage implicating their daughter and her friends as menaces to each other.

Once we reached an impasse in the quest for a Jasmine-and-Elise peace accord, we moved on to our next form of entertainment, prank calling cute boys in our class. As soon as Kerr Oliver's adorable voice answered the line, the entire set of girls screamed and hung up the phone.

Kerr's dad pushed *69, which connected the line to its previous caller. Mr. Oliver told us he was going to call the police if we ever called his son again, so we slammed down the receiver and ran screaming up and down the stairs until we exhausted ourselves.

When it was time for bed, we lined up our sleeping bags in the family den, but inevitably, someone was hungry and went into the kitchen for a midnight snack. In this instance, Elise was the person who rushed back into the den screaming that there were shadowy burglar figures in the backyard. I had to calm and reassure her by turning on the light and explaining that they were merely stone statues depicting French country life that Mom had ordered from furniture market in Dallas.

Finally, everyone drifted to sleep, and the excitement was over until 2 a.m., when I sat straight up hollering in pain from swimmer's ear, the product of too much pool water getting clogged in my ear ducts. Kristen frantically scurried for Mom, who appeared with magic drops that had to drain into each ear for several minutes to take effect.

My friends' moms always arrived before 8 a.m. Saturday morning. My friends joked that I was such a sound sleeper that they had to stick a buzzing alarm clock next to my head to wake me up after a slumber party.

But without fail, I was back to my school persona by Monday morning. My teachers commented on my reserved nature and asked if I were this shy at home. Every one of the girls started laughing and relaying different stories about our prank calls to boys, my running up and down the stairs screaming with a soda in hand and their holding the alarm next to my face to get me out of bed Saturday morning.

Mrs. Clayton gave me a searching look, as if to ask, "Ashley, can this be true?"

I blushed and smiled a demure grin. Who was she going to believe, them or me?

"Friday night?" I said. "Oh, it was just a few of my close friends who stopped by with their sleeping bags for some pizza and good old-fashioned home movies."

THE BABYSITTER

The best babysitter I ever had was a British college student named Annemarie. She played games with Kristen Bennett and me and taught us to ballroom dance. She was silly and kind, so we were devastated when she graduated from college and moved home to England.

Somehow, my parents managed to locate the world's worst babysitter as their next hire. Mona Ingefoot was the middle-aged daughter of sweet, elderly Ava Ingefoot, who lived next door to our family. Mona's daughter Carrie was quiet and sweet like her grandmother but never available to babysit. The kindness gene must have been recessive and skipped Mona altogether.

A couple of minutes after she watched my parents' car reverse from the driveway, Mona planted herself on the couch and began dishing out orders to Robin, Kristen and me. "Go to the kitchen and get me another slice of pizza," she said.

When I stood up to go to the kitchen, she snapped her fingers and pointed to the ground, which was her nonverbal way of telling me to crawl under the big-screen television so as not to obstruct her view with my body. So I obediently crawled under the screen, inching forward limb by limb like a reptile so I didn't block her view of the game show she was watching on my parents' tab.

Mona despised Robin and me but tolerated Kristen because, as Mona said, "She was a premie." Once, as the three of us played board games on the den floor, Mona said, without provocation, "Ashley and Robin, go to your rooms."

Robin and I had to remain isolated in our own bedrooms until our parents returned, while Kristen was allowed to sit in the den under the condition that she must play the board game alone and in silence. According to Kristen, Mona passed the time by popping pizza in her cavernous mouth and scratching her fuzzy socks against the ottoman.

Mona was the master of sucking up to my parents, so when I woefully told Mom and Dad about her horrible true nature, they rolled back their heads in laughter and disbelief. They truly thought Kristen and I were exaggerating. What kind of cruel babysitter would make good kids like us crawl under the TV screen?

Our pent-up frustration stewed from within until the day Sue Bennett hired Brooke Sparks, a high-school student, to babysit us at Kristen's house. By that time, both of our minds boiled over with ideas. Kristen and I gathered some items, a ski mask, ski goggles with green-tinted lens and a wool ski cap, from Sue's closet.

I was all set to play the role of Louisa, Kristen's blind-and-deaf foreign exchange student, who, oddly enough, could somehow communicate with Kristen through a sisterly language we had forged during my time in America. Though the result sounded like two whales breathing through their blowholes, Kristen and I were fully convinced that Brooke would buy into our scam.

All went well until Kristen threw Gak, a blob of green goo that left a slimy film on anything it touched, onto the den ceiling. All three of us looked up, four if you count blind-and-deaf Louisa, whose gaze followed the blob as it slowly dropped from the ceiling to the floor.

"I thought you said she couldn't see anything," Brooke said.

Clearly, she didn't think we were as adorable and amusing as we imagined ourselves to be. Our second scheme was to make Brooke buy two tickets, even though she was the only guest, to the confetti parade we hosted in the Bennetts' long hallway.

Kristen and I tossed small pieces of confetti everywhere, trying our best to jam particles into the carpet's crevices with our feet. We cartwheeled down the hallway until we had exhausted all of our energy. At that point, we dismissed Brooke form the parade and hid on the top shelf of the hallway closet until clean-up time, when we explained that it was part of the babysitter's job description to vacuum the confetti off the floor and wipe the leftover, green Gak film from the ceilings and walls.

Kristen and I really felt like we were getting away with something, failing to realize that we'd missed the mark, since Mona Ingefoot was nowhere in sight.

WALT DISNEY WORLD

Our Walt Disney World family obsession began when I was 2 and Robin was 6. Together, we watched every animated Disney movie and every television special about the theme parks. Our parents bought every Disney travel book, and Dad read Steve Birnbaum's guides in such detail that Robin thought Steve was even more famous than Mickey and Minnie Mouse.

We have a photo from our first Disney vacation of Robin and me, both of us wearing Japanese kimonos and karate-inspired headbands at Epcot Center. Mom and Dad pushed me in a stroller that trip, until Robin got tired and asked, "How come she gets to ride in the stroller?" After that, Robin, age 6, rode in my stroller, and Dad carried me on his shoulders the whole day.

By the time I was 4, Mom bought me a red-and-white, polka-dot dress, embroidered with Minnie Mouse's face and signature front and center. I loved it so much that I wore the dress every day during our second Disney vacation.

After our trip, I wore it so often that it finally faded and ripped, and then I insisted on wearing it again until Mom finally had to make the dress disappear like a handful of Tinker Bell's fairy dust. Robin left that trip in hysterics because, though she had met Mickey and Minnie, she hadn't seen Steve Birnbaum of Disney travel-guide fame.

I left the trip equally as panicked after I met the real Minnie Mouse. I was so timid around her that she played along, hiding her head behind her hands in a game of peekaboo. Back and forth we went, my face hidden behind the safety of Mom's skirt and Minnie's face hidden behind her large, white glove hands. I was pretty sure I liked the embroidered Minnie on my faded dress much better than I liked her living, breathing counterpart.

My dad loves to tell the story about the time we stayed at the Holiday Inn. It was before we knew the mainstream Disney sidekicks like Pluto, Goofy and the Seven Dwarfs. Robin and I were so enamored with Holiday Inn's version, the Holiday Hound, that we followed him around everywhere he went during our morning buffet breakfasts. Dad was impressed that we had twice the fun with the Holiday Hound for half the price of an official Disney hotel.

Thankfully, Dad splurged a little during our next stint in Orlando, letting us stay at the Contemporary Resort. I remember sitting on the bed of our hotel room, which had a TV station devoted exclusively to Disney music videos, and watching "When You Wish Upon a Star" as the lyrics scrolled onscreen. It was the saddest, sweetest, most beautiful song I had ever heard. I looked over at Dad, who was sitting on the edge of the bed next to mine, and saw tears streaming down his face.

The next morning at breakfast, I became enamored with the tiny, paper milk cartons that peel open on one side. I insisted to Mom that we must take the Contemporary Resort's tradition home and serve Disney-themed milk cartons and Florida oranges on our very own breakfast buffet, all of the items shaped like Mickey Mouse. There would be Mickey pancakes, Mickey waffles, and even our hash browns would bear a resemblance to Mickey's face.

I spent a lot of time daydreaming about such things during the bus ride from our hotel to the Magic Kingdom, which always seemed like the slow train from San Diego to Boston. Once we made it inside the theme park, Mom and Dad wanted to ride the wooden locomotive train around the whole park. Either that or the Monorail, said to be the "fastest ride at Disney," though it seemed to inch along compared to Space Mountain.

While our parents visited the Disney information center and made plans to watch the historical film, Robin and I groaned. How did they manage instantly to locate the only boring parts of Walt Disney World? Robin and I begged for our freedom and moved on to the more adventurous side of the park, like Splash Mountain, where we vowed to get as wet as we possibly could.

Sometimes, we intersected with Mom and Dad, who planted themselves behind the roped sidewalks of Main Street to claim their seats for the parades. Robin and I waved and ran past all of the statuesque people in Mickey ears, taking advantage of shorter ride lines and stopping off for cotton candy and Mickey-shaped ice-cream sandwiches along the way.

It was at Epcot Center where I made my first-ever credit-card purchase at the Japan boutique. As the young Japanese clerk slid my card and handed me my receipt, Dad kept saying, "konichiwa," thinking it meant "thank you," when really it meant "hello." She smiled politely but looked at him with a perplexed stare.

Dad really lived it up during our annual Disney adventures. We have a photo of Dad and me with the malts we were sharing. There were two malts with two straws, both of them in Dad's mouth as I grinned for the camera, opting to give him the calories.

One time, after a parade, I noticed an elderly, uniformed man, who was a Disney employee, sweeping trash and whistling a chipper tune as he wiped up gummy bears and confetti giblets on Main Street. I suggested to Dad that he should consider retiring at Walt Disney World, where he could begin a second career as a trash collector. Dad acted sort of insulted, but I was serious. Walt Disney World was already his second home, so he might as well get paid to be there.

Every trip, on our last night at the theme park, we had to drag a mopey Dad past the exits after the fireworks show. At the Orlando airport, Dad got sad just like all of the other kids in line for the flights back to their hometowns. He commiserated with them, saying, "I can't wait to come back to the happiest place on Earth either."

It was then that I realized that our childhood trips to Walt Disney World were more for Dad's benefit than mine and Robin's. I could just picture Dad, long after Robin and I were grown, stretching back on a Disney park bench, maybe he'd be 90 years old, smiling contentedly as he waved to groups of families, saying, "Have a magical day."